A Body in the Backyard

A Myrtle Clover Cozy Mystery, Volume 4

Elizabeth Spann Craig

Published by Elizabeth Spann Craig, 2019.

A BODY IN THE BACKYARD

First edition. August 7, 2019.

Written by Elizabeth Spann Craig.

For my children and in memory of my grandmothers.

Chapter One

Myrtle's ancient yardman opened up the back door, not bothering to wipe his boots on the mat, and trampled through the kitchen and living room all the way to Myrtle's front door.

Dusty *was* completely incompetent as a yardman, but this degree of sloppiness was a stretch, even for him. His wife, Puddin, was equally appalled. She was resentfully slapping a dust rag at Myrtle's coffee table when she stopped and stared at the red mud tracking in behind her husband. "Hey!" she shouted. "I ain't cleaning that up, Dusty! You get back here! You can clean up yer own messes."

Dusty was reaching for the door handle when Myrtle bellowed, "Your shoes, Dusty! And, you haven't finished the backyard yet! It still looks like a jungle back there."

Dusty glared at Myrtle, and gave a mumbling mutter in response.

"I wish you wouldn't use tobacco products on the job, Dusty. For one thing, it means you'll die and then I'll have to find myself yet another sorry yardman. For another, I can't hear a word you say. It sounded like you said 'dead body,' for heaven's sake."

He scowled at her before carefully pushing the wad of chewing tobacco to the side with his tongue. "Dead body! In yer backyard. Getting Red."

Dusty yanked open Myrtle's front door and started loping across her gnome-filled front yard toward Red's house. Red was Myrtle's son, neighbor, and chief of police of the small town of Bradley, North Carolina. He was insufferable when it came to getting into Myrtle's personal business and he wasn't at all fond of Myrtle's hobby of crime fighting.

Considering Dusty would have reported the crime in mere seconds, Myrtle had to act fast if she were to investigate this murder in her own backyard before being pushed out of the way.

Puddin was crossing herself, although Myrtle knew her to be a lifelong Baptist. Her white face was especially pasty after the shock of the body outside. She also seemed to be muttering something under her breath—possibly a strange variation of the Lord's Prayer. She saw that Myrtle was on her way out to the body and hissed to her, "Close his eyes up, Miz Myrtle!"

"Why should I do that? I can't interfere with the body, Puddin. Red will have my head on a silver platter if I do," said Myrtle.

"If you don't close them eyes, he'll find somebody to take with him on his journey to the afterlife!"

"Puddin, I'm done with your nonsense today. I swear; I never know what foolishness is going to come out of your mouth next. Tell you what. Just for today, you can pour yourself a small drink from my fridge. That should help pull you together enough to finish my dusting. I've got stuff to do, okay?" Then Myrtle quickly popped into her backyard.

There, right in front of her azalea bushes and near her birdfeeder was the body. He looked to be a young man. Well, he was probably thirty-five or thirty-six. Was that considered young? It certainly seemed like it to octogenarian Myrtle. He was handsome in sort of a cheap-looking way, aside from the fact that part of his head was bashed in, which clearly was what put him in this predicament of being dead in Myrtle's bushes.

Most vexingly, about a yard away from the young/youngish man, one of her favorite gnomes lay on his side with a chipped base. It was the Viking gnome with a fierce expression and a sword and who mysteriously held a pipe. Myrtle was certain that the Vikings didn't smoke. But, the gnome had a lot of personality. Of course, now it was a murder weapon and would probably be taken away and studied. A bad day for the Viking gnome. She frowned. On closer inspection, it looked like the side the gnome had landed on might be cracked and broken. She sighed.

Were there any clues? She saw no footprints but Dusty's. It looked as though her bushes had been trampled through. Had the murderer hid in the bushes, jumped out, and walloped the victim on the head?

Who on earth *was* this man?

On the plus side, he appeared to be scaring off the squirrels that kept raiding Myrtle's feeder.

She jumped as a deep voice called out, "What have you done now, Mama?"

Red. She sniffed. "Not a blessed thing. Although you'd think that I wouldn't find bodies in my backyard, with the chief of police living across the street. What's the world coming to?"

Red studied the body. "This guy seems vaguely familiar looking. Can't place him, though." He sighed. "So what's your relationship with him, Mama? He cheat you at Bingo? Call you Sugar? I know how you hate being called Sugar."

"It's inappropriate and disrespectful...disgraceful, really...for people to call senior citizens by pet names. And no, I don't know who this fellow is," said Myrtle.

"Looks like your gnome took him out," said Red, nodding at the Viking. "Sure you didn't have a grudge against the guy?"

"If I did, I sure wouldn't have used my Viking to kill him. Nor broken it. He's one of my favorites," said Myrtle. "Isn't he one of yours?"

Red said stiffly, "I try not to look at your gnomes, Mama."

The garden gnomes made their appearance in Myrtle's front and back yards when Red had done something to drive Myrtle up the wall. This was well known to all in the town of Bradley. Since he disliked the gnomes so much, and lived so close to Myrtle, dragging out a hundred of them was well worth the effort and always made her point perfectly clear. This time the gnomes were occupying her yard because of Red's insistence that she consider using a walker. There was *no* need for a walker. Myrtle's cane worked perfectly.

"Do you have any idea how long he's been lying here?" asked Red, crouching down on his knees and peering at the body.

The fact that she hadn't seen any of the drama when it took place in her backyard was giving Myrtle heartburn. "I didn't notice him. Dusty was the one who found him." It pained her to admit this.

"Do you think he might have been out in your yard since last night, even?" asked Red.

Myrtle reconstructed the evening. "Well, I was out in the backyard, feeding Pasha, right after it got dark. Maybe around nine o'clock. I don't recollect seeing a body there then. But Pasha was acting funny. Hissing at shadows, fur up on her back, that kind of thing."

"Considering Pasha is a feral animal, I'm guessing you didn't put too much stock in that behavior," said Red dryly.

"She's a lovely cat, Red, but yes, sometimes she turns into a wild thing. I blame it on the moon cycles."

"If that's what you want to blame it on, Mama. Does the cat have all its shots? It looks like it wants to attack people all the time."

"Her shots are completely current," said Myrtle. She frowned. "Can we get back to the body? Have you contacted the state police about this?"

"I put a call out while I was walking over. Didn't tell them the body was in my mother's own yard." Red ran a hand through the red hair that gave him his nickname. It seemed to be getting whiter each time Myrtle saw him. He tried to get back on track with his questioning. "So you didn't see him on the ground when you fed Pasha."

"But the cat was acting oddly then," stressed Myrtle.

Red ignored her interjection. "And you didn't notice him out the window when you got up this morning. How about the middle of the night? Did you have your usual insomnia last night?"

She had. She'd felt as if it was time to get up for the day in the middle of the night. And she'd gone for a walk down the street. Not that she was going to tell Red that. A stroll at two a.m. would likely mean a renewed campaign for the dreaded walker.

"I was awake last night so I should have heard something. Well, I guess there was a pretty long period of time when I decided to take a hot shower. Sometimes I like to do that to loosen up my muscles and clear my sinuses with the steam. Then after that, I was awake until three. I didn't see anything, though," said Myrtle.

There was a discreet, gentlemanly cough behind them and Red and Myrtle turned to see Myrtle's neighbor, Miles. He looked from the body on the ground back to Red and Myrtle and gave an uncertain smile. "Is there some kind of trouble?"

Red sighed. "I'm just trying to ascertain if Mama finally flipped her lid and killed somebody just to have a crime to investigate. I'm not sure what lengths she'll go to in order to prevent boredom."

Myrtle gave him a repressive look. "I'd do no such thing." She turned to Miles. "Dusty found a body in my yard this morning. We're trying to figure out who he is, when he died and who was responsible."

"If Dusty and Puddin are here with all this going on, that might explain why Puddin is in your front yard muttering to Pasha and holding a cross up in front of her," said Miles dryly. "While swigging sherry, I might add."

"Oh, Puddin thinks Pasha is a witch. Always utter foolishness from Puddin, you know," said Myrtle. "I'd go rescue Pasha, but she can stand up for herself." Pasha was ferocious if she didn't like you.

Miles shivered. Pasha didn't particularly like him, either.

Red said, "You don't have any idea who this fellow is, do you, Miles? And did you notice anything strange last night?"

Miles walked closer, stepping gingerly on the grass as if to avoid tampering with clues. He stopped, leaned in, and then stood up straight. He turned back to Red and Myrtle. "That," he said, removing his steel-framed glasses and wiping them, "is my cousin Charles."

Chapter Two

They stared at him.

"Your cousin Charles is dead in my yard?" asked Myrtle. "How—well, how careless of you, Miles!"

"He's not my responsibility," protested Miles. "I haven't seen him in years, as a matter of fact. And he's a grown man, for heaven's sake. I haven't the foggiest idea why he might be dead in your yard. I didn't see or hear anything last night. I turned in fairly early last night and even put my earplugs in, because Pasha was wailing at one point and acting peculiar. But that's not really out of the ordinary."

They all looked quietly out on the scene in front of them for a moment. Myrtle's yard was filled with gnomes, feeders, and colorful azaleas—and a body blocking the path that led down the wooded hill to her small dock on the lake.

"I didn't even know you had a Cousin Charles," said Myrtle.

Miles put his glasses back on and looked at the body thoughtfully. "He's not the sort of cousin that you claim."

"Any ideas about why he might be dead in Mama's backyard?" asked Red. "I'd love to have some theories by the time the state police get over here. Particularly since my mother is involved."

"I'm no more involved than Dusty!" said Myrtle. "I just happened to *host* the dead body. Dusty actually discovered it. And good luck getting any sense out of him."

Miles cleared his throat. "If I had to guess, I'd imagine that he was here trying to get money out of me. Just a guess."

Myrtle was impressed that Miles had ventured into the realm of the imagination enough to come up with a possible scenario. "That's so fanciful of you, Miles."

Red was jotting down notes. "So this Charles—did he usually take on a lot of debt then?"

"I don't know about his debts, but I do know that he's one of those people who is terminally in a hole. He grew up here in Bradley, but he's been gone since he graduated from high school, I think. I'm not real sure he's ever kept down a job for more than a month at a time, but his mother always made allowances for it in the same breath she mentioned it: 'Oh, Charles can't ever find a job that lets him really show off his talents.' If Charles had any talents, they had to be related to procrastination and deviousness," said Miles.

"His mother?" asked Myrtle. "Do you have an aunt around here too? Really, Miles! Any other relatives I should know about?" She glanced around her as if Miles's kin might start popping out from behind gnomes or falling from the sky. "A crazed granny in the attic, with a spinning wheel perhaps?"

Red rolled his eyes. "I wouldn't be talking about crazy grannies if I were you, Mama. Besides, you're the one with all the relatives. You're related to most of the town. Probably related to Cousin Charles yourself."

"Well, that's typical when you live in a small town. People intermarry," said Myrtle.

"I do have an aunt nearby, but she doesn't live in Bradley. She's over in Simonton," said Miles.

"Oh, so she lives far away, then. Like ten whole minutes from here," said Myrtle. "And aren't you a bit long in the tooth to have aunts wandering around? She must be hundreds of years old."

"This aunt is actually younger than I am," said Miles stiffly.

"How positively Gothic!" said Myrtle.

"Mama, give it up. So Miles, are you in contact with her often?" asked Red.

"Not so much. Actually, she's a rather unpleasant person to be around. I did check in with her when I moved to Bradley, but other than that, I've only talked to her on the phone a few times." Miles sighed. "I guess I'll have to get in touch with her about this." He didn't sound like he was looking forward to the meeting.

Myrtle was still stuck on the fact that Miles had hidden facets to his life. "I thought you just moved here from Atlanta because this is such a retirement magnet with the lake and everything." Bradley, North Carolina, population fifteen-hundred, wasn't really a magnet of any kind. But there was a nice little lake, which tended to draw a nice-sized retirement-age populace to the town.

"That was part of it. But the reason I was so familiar with the area was because I had family here," said Miles. "My uncle and aunt lived here until my uncle died and my aunt moved to Creighton."

Myrtle's back door slammed and Dusty moseyed up to them in his unhurried way. He studied Charles. "It's a body, all right," he said, apparently looking for someone to agree with him.

Red said, "You haven't seen this guy around town have you, Dusty?"

Dusty squinted at the body. "Yeah, seen him fightin' at the poker game." He nodded at Red. "You seen him too."

Red frowned and moved closer to the body, studying it. "Well, I'll be doggoned. That's the guy in the fight I broke up last weekend."

"As I said, not the kind of cousin you claim," said Miles.

Red was trying to remember the incident. "He was fighting with Lee Woosley. I didn't even take their names down or anything, but I told them to knock it off or I was going to have to lock them up for the night. They sort of slunk off, as I recall. I didn't recognize Charles and he said he was visiting." He looked at the body again. "Well, I'll be."

Dusty announced to Myrtle, "I'm taking Puddin back home now. She asked if you'd closed the man's eyelids."

"You will *not* be taking Puddin back home now! You haven't finished mowing or weed-eating my yard yet, Dusty. And I'm sure Puddin hasn't done squat since you found this body," said Myrtle.

"Think you'd rather have me take her home," said Dusty. "She's talking about scattering your fireplace ashes around for protection from spirits."

"What? That's not even a real superstition....that's something Puddin just made up." Puddin and Dusty would do anything to get out of work. Once they left Myrtle's house, she'd have the dickens of a time getting them to come back and finish the job they started. She hurried to the house before Puddin dumped ashes all over the place. Really, it was like dealing with very slow and magically-minded children.

Red was explaining to Dusty why he couldn't disturb the body before the state police came and Dusty was arguing back that Charles was looking for somebody to take with him. It all made Myrtle's head hurt.

Puddin was already in the fireplace when Myrtle bellowed, "Stop! Stop it, Puddin! Unless you want to clean up every single bit of ash, get out of the fireplace."

Puddin looked sullenly at her, but there was a hint of genuine fear in her face. "Always something dangerous going on here. This place is hexed."

"Hexed by poor housekeeping and slothfulness, maybe. Puddin, you haven't even finished up the little bit of work you started! What about my kitchen? You said you'd clean my floor in there," said Myrtle.

"I'm not cleaning with them evil spirits around," said Puddin, giving a defiant bob of her head.

Myrtle muttered darkly under her breath. "I'm getting too old to clean my floors and do heavy cleaning, Puddin."

Red walked in from the backyard. "But not too old to chase criminals down?"

"Crime fighting never means I have to stoop down. Cleaning baseboards and scrubbing bathrooms means stooping," said Myrtle.

Puddin was collecting her cleaning supplies. And some of Myrtle's. "That furniture polish is mine, Puddin."

"Ain't neither! I brought it from home," said Puddin.

"Brought it from home because you took it from me last time," said Myrtle. Puddin was supposed to use her own supplies, but it never ended up that way.

Puddin put the polish back, resentfully, then made a jab at Myrtle that she knew would get at her, "By the way, your neighbor is out there. Erma." She looked gleeful at Myrtle's dismay.

Myrtle stomped over to the window to peer out. Sure enough, her donkey-faced, nosy neighbor was standing in her yard, gaping at her front door. "What's keeping her from ringing my doorbell?" mused Myrtle.

"That witch. It's on your front porch. Evil spirits," intoned Puddin, taking a detour into the occult again.

"Pasha?" This was one reason why Myrtle loved that cat so much. "The darling."

"Need you to move it," said Puddin, holding her cleaning bucket with both hands. "I can't leave while it's out there."

And Erma couldn't come in with Pasha out there. It sounded like Pasha needed to stay put.

Red said in his authoritative voice, "You can't go anywhere, Puddin. I've got to take Dusty's statement. The state police might want to question him, too."

"What!" Puddin looked alarmed. "I need to go home. How long will that all take?"

"By the time they get a unit over here, it might be almost an hour," said Red. "But they're on their way."

"I'll miss my show!" said Puddin.

"Might as well clean while you're here," said Myrtle with satisfaction. So, Puddin's urgent desire to escape Myrtle's house had all been due to her soap opera after all.

Myrtle's phone started ringing and she peered out the window again. "Erma's gone in, so that call is probably from her." She looked at the ringing phone distastefully. "Puddin, if you're not going to clean, you can at least answer the phone for me. There's sure to be plenty of calls once the state police cars and forensics truck show up."

Puddin glared at the phone.

"And try to be gracious," said Myrtle.

Puddin slouched over to the phone and picked up the receiver while drawing herself up as tall and proper as her short, dumpy stature could manage. "Miz Myrtle's residence." She listened for a second, and then rolled her eyes at Myrtle, slumping again. It was apparently Erma, as Myrtle had figured. She could hear the nasal voice from where she stood. "Miz Myrtle is busy right now. That's right. There's a dead man in the backyard. Yep." She held the phone away from her head and squawking could be heard from yards away. "Got to go," said Puddin and she unceremoniously dropped the phone back on the receiver as the squawking continued.

It immediately started ringing again and Myrtle walked over, lifted up the receiver, hung up, then took it off the hook. "That should stop all those busybodies."

Of course it didn't. By the time the state police and the forensic team had gone over her backyard with a fine-toothed comb and questioned her hapless yardman, the entire town of Bradley was buzzing about Myrtle Clover's dead body. And half the town was standing in either Miles's or Erma's yard to view the proceedings.

Myrtle was pleased as punch that her house was a temporary command center for an investigation. Usually she was shooed away from crime scenes. This time the crime scene surrounded her. From what she could gather in snatches of conversation, the body had been in her yard since late last night—after dark, for sure. Miles's Cousin Charles had indeed been killed by a blow to the head from her Viking gnome. And there didn't seem to be any real physical evidence that indicated who the killer was.

Red said, "Dusty and Puddin, we're all done talking with y'all. You're free to head home."

Puddin quickly picked up her cleaning bucket again and she and Dusty moved out of the house quicker than Myrtle had ever seen them move before. She watched them through the window as they left and noticed her boss at the small local newspaper, Sloan Jones, taking pictures of them as they left. Dusty looked as grouchy as ever, but Puddin managed a simpering pose as she clutched her bucket.

Neighbors appeared to be asking them questions and she saw Puddin put the bucket down and enjoy her few minutes in the limelight. From Myrtle's interpretation of the pantomime, it appeared that her story centered around Pasha the Witch and evil spirits. Her audience watched with wide-eyed rapture until Dusty yanked her by the arm and they climbed into their aging truck.

The police finally finished up. Myrtle's interview had been woefully short since she'd seen and heard nothing. Miles's hadn't been much better, since he could only identify the victim and give a very vague background on him. He hadn't seen or heard anything, either. "Do I need to visit my aunt and tell her the news?" he asked in a rather stressed voice.

"No, I think it would be better if the police took that on," said Red with a sigh. "We'll want to talk to her about Charles and why he was in town, her last conversation with him—-that kind of thing. But thanks."

Miles looked relieved. "Wonderful. I mean—oh, good. Yes. Well, I can delay talking to my aunt a while then. Although I suppose I'll have to give some kind of funeral lunch or family reception or something like that. The family plot is here in Bradley."

Myrtle's wheels were spinning. "I know what a drain that would be on you, Miles. Especially since you're not fond of your family."

"I didn't say I wasn't fond of all of them...."

"So I'd be happy to host a reception here. At my house. Near the spot where Cousin Charles spent his final minutes," said Myrtle, looking reverent.

Chapter Three

Red was taken aback. "A reception? With...food?"

"Of course with food! This is the South, Red. People want food when they're grieving. People *expect* food when they're grieving," said Myrtle.

"They don't expect the kind of food you cook, Mama." Red and Miles exchanged grim looks.

"I think they'll be delighted," said Myrtle. She frowned. "Are you trying to be ugly about my cooking again?"

"I'm just saying that, unless you want a whole bunch more dead bodies on your property, I'd consider getting your reception catered," said Red. "Okay, that's it for me. Miles, I'll be getting back in touch with you soon I'm sure. I better head over to the station and fill out paperwork." He headed to the front door.

Myrtle said quickly, "Better watch out. Erma has left her lair and it looked like she wanted to pester somebody."

Red peered out the front window at the sea of gnomes. "You know, Mama, you're not exactly a prize for a neighbor either."

"I certainly am!"

"I'm your neighbor, so I think I'm well-qualified to give an opinion on your adequacy in that regard," said Red.

"Miles, back me up," said Myrtle.

But Miles looked like he was suffering a nightmarish flashback of some kind. Myrtle trusted it had nothing to do with her worthiness as a neighbor.

Red said, "At any rate, it looks like Erma has given up and gone back inside."

"Pasha is such a *good* cat," said Myrtle, pleased.

"If you say so," said Red. "And Mama, I'm not sure what's going on with the murder in your backyard, but please make sure to keep your doors locked. We just don't know what we're dealing with right now. And for heaven's sake, don't play detective. All I need is for you to stick your nose into the middle of this stuff and muck up my investigation." He walked out the front door and strode down the front walkway.

Myrtle hurried after him, thumping the walkway with her cane. "I don't make a habit of mucking up investigations," said Myrtle, making her voice as frigid as she possibly could. "As you know, I solve the mysteries. I help you out."

Red shook his head. "Maybe you've been lucky, Mama. Maybe you've stumbled into stuff by accident. Regardless, you need to keep out of it this time. You only just finished getting over that really dangerous virus, followed by an infection."

"What dangerous virus? You mean the sniffles?" Myrtle gave what she hoped was a careless, scoffing laugh. "It takes more than a drippy nose to take me down, Red."

"It *was* more than a drippy nose. It got into your chest, as you well know, and you ended up with bronchitis."

"Just a little cough," said Myrtle. This was all starting to make her feel grouchy.

"Just a little cough, or another reminder that you're in your late-eighties? You're no spring chicken, you know. Leave the investigating to the pros."

It was lovely being told she was too old to do things.

Red's toddler son, Jack, bolted out of their house and saw the lawn-mower that Dusty was packing up into his dilapidated truck. Jack was currently fascinated by anything with an engine. "I mow!" he half-com-manded, half-begged his father, pointing at the beat-up mower.

Red picked up Jack and gave him a hug. "Can't do it, buddy," he said, swinging the boy around and putting him back down again. "You're too little to mow the grass. But I'd love for you to help me out in another ten years."

Red hurried inside the house. Myrtle looked wryly at Jack. "So I'm too old and you're too young."

Jack furrowed his brow and pointed again at the mower.

"Lucky for you, I've figured out the cure for these types of insults and rejections." Myrtle fished in her dress pocket. "Chocolate."

They beamed at each other. Myrtle broke the chocolate bar in half and Jack put a big chunk in his mouth, then gave her a chocolaty grin.

"Now I need you to run inside, little man. I've got some stuff to do at my house." Myrtle watched him run safely back inside and headed home.

Miles was making motions like he wanted to leave. "Have a seat, Miles," said Myrtle. "After all, that must have been a huge shock for you."

Miles sighed with resignation and obediently took a seat but said, "Not particularly. I can't make myself feel even very concerned about it."

He settled into Myrtle's cushy sofa. Myrtle sat opposite him in an upright armchair and leaned forward. "Okay. Now, let's hear all about Cousin Charles."

Miles blinked at her from behind his glasses. "As I told the police, I really don't...."

"And I don't want that vague story you gave the cops, either. I want the dirt on the guy who ended up pushing up daisies in my backyard."

Miles sighed. "I don't have any dirt, Myrtle. I don't even know the man. I didn't want to, either. He was many years younger than me, obviously and always sounded somewhat unsavory, no matter how my aunt bragged about him."

"Unsavory. Now we're getting somewhere! What qualities made him unsavory?" asked Myrtle.

"Oh, I don't know. Sometimes one of my other cousins would email me and dish on Charles. Things she'd heard. Apparently he'd struggled with substance abuse, for one," said Miles.

"So he was a druggie. Good. That's something solid we can work with. What else?" asked Myrtle.

"Maybe not a druggie. Maybe an alcoholic. I'm not really sure. At any rate, if there were any hint from my aunt about Charles's issues, she'd quickly blame them on a vast government conspiracy of some kind. She always made excuses for her son. I just tuned her out," said Miles.

"Mmm. Okay. Well, people do desperate things to get their next fix, right? Even if that's a bottle of whiskey. So, let's move on. Who do you think wanted to kill him?" asked Myrtle.

"Well, I don't really know that. Since I didn't know him." Miles frowned at Myrtle.

"Let me rephrase that. Who wanted to kill him...besides you?" asked Myrtle.

"What? I didn't want to kill Cousin Charles! I said I didn't even know him," said Miles, looking as excitable as it was possible for him to look.

"Except that he wanted to take money from you. I believe you to be fairly tight-fisted when it comes to money. You want to spend it all on good scotch and collector-editions of Hemingway. Not to support your clingy, drug-using cousin," said Myrtle.

"I certainly am not! Not like that, I mean. And I have no idea why my cousin was nearby...I'm only guessing that he was trying to find me to ask for money." Miles glared at her. "It could be that he was trying to break into your house and look for money or something to sell on the street. In that case, maybe *you* killed him with the gnome, in self-defense. Or, to have something to do. We all know how bored you get and how much you like investigating mysteries."

Myrtle spluttered trying to formulate a response and Miles stood up, smoothing out imaginary wrinkles from his carefully pressed trousers. "And now I really must be going. I'll need to talk with my family about this tragic death." He stood to leave in a huff.

Myrtle looked thoughtfully at him. It was funny how death had such interesting effects on people. "Oh, Miles, have a seat. I need about forty-five good minutes to just relax and gather my thoughts."

Miles brightened. "Are you proposing that we watch our show?"

"I sure am. *Tomorrow's Promise* just finished taping for today. We can eat some graham crackers and peanut butter and watch our soap," said Myrtle with satisfaction.

"Just as long as you remember that you're not to tell anyone that I *have* a soap. You got me hooked on it, that's all."

"They're very addicting shows," said Myrtle, knowingly.

"Didn't it scare you? Finding a body in your yard like that?" asked Red's wife, Elaine. That afternoon, Myrtle walked across their quiet street to Red's house to visit with her daughter-in-law and grandson. Toddler Jack played on the floor making truck noises and pushing toy cars around on the floor.

Myrtle shook her head. "Not a bit. But I didn't find the body, technically. Dusty did."

Elaine reached out and absently pulled a toy car out of Jack's mouth. "Oh, that must have been interesting. Dusty's always scowling when I see him. Did he even look surprised when he found the body? Worried? Upset?"

"Of course not. He was as ornery as anything. He acted more concerned that body removal was somehow in the yardman job description. Kept fussing that it wasn't fair that there was a body out there when he already had to weed-whack around all the gnomes. You know." Myrtle rolled her eyes.

"Was Puddin with him when he found the body?" asked Elaine.

"No. But you should have known the answer to that question already. If Puddin had found the body, you'd have heard her screaming from all the way over here," said Myrtle. Jack stood up and handed her a very wet toy police car and Myrtle gingerly picked it up and made vroom, vroom noises.

"You know, I always thought that Bradley was such a peaceful little town," said Elaine thoughtfully. "It's got the tree-lined, quiet streets, the quaint shops. No national chains anywhere. A beautiful lake. And here we are with bodies fairly littering the city all the time."

"It's peaceful, Elaine, I promise. Other towns have a whole lot more crime than this. You know the kinds of cases that Red is usually working on," said Myrtle.

Elaine nodded. "There's Mrs. Hatter, who always calls about the kids who trespass in her yard and cut her clothesline. Nuisance calls from the Smiths because their neighbors always play loud music next door and it drives them crazy."

"And don't forget his big task as chief of police," said Myrtle. "Putting up the town of Bradley's Christmas decorations each November."

"For Red, that's the hardest part of his job," said Elaine with a laugh. "He's convinced some miscreant sneaks into the Town Hall each summer and maliciously tangles up all the lights."

They chuckled over this, and Jack, watching them, chuckled too. Myrtle reached over to squeeze the boy in a hug

Elaine said, "But it's not all sunshine and roses, Myrtle. Red had an incident just the other day and I was with him."

"Did he now?" asked Myrtle absently as Jack clutched at her leg and drove a toy car up her easy-care navy slacks.

"Yes." Elaine stood up and moved across the room to a desk that was fairly overflowing with paper. She started shuffling through the stacks. Myrtle winced as she watched her. Elaine must have a new hobby. Elaine took on new hobbies with determination and poured much of her considerable energy into the pursuit, exhausting everyone around her. Sadly, she'd yet to hit on something that she was truly gifted in doing.

Elaine stopped pawing through the pile of papers, and abruptly turned and looked at Myrtle with an enthusiastic expression that Myrtle knew well. "Did you know that I've taken up photography?" she asked with excitement lacing her voice.

Photography. Excellent! No being subjected to painstakingly created and horrid watercolors or oils. No mysterious-looking sculptures or indecipherable charcoal sketches. "No, you didn't tell me you'd taken up photography. Are you enjoying it?"

"It's fantastic," said Elaine, searching through the pile again while Jack toddled over to drive his car on her foot. "I love the feeling that I'm looking at the world through a lens. It makes me closer to the world and farther away at the same time."

Was she any good, though? Or was this going to be another one of those endeavors where Red and Myrtle gave insincere but well-meant praise on disastrous projects? She had that old familiar feeling of trepidation.

"Now I'm just starting out," said Elaine, turning around with some pictures in her hand, "so these will be a little blurry."

Great.

"But ordinarily I'm shooting still-life kinds of compositions, so this action shot was new for me. It's just to prove that we do have stuff going on in Bradley after all," said Elaine. She handed the pictures to Myrtle.

There was Cousin Charles in a vibrant pre-murdered state, in the act of punching Lee Woosley in the face at a poker game.

Elaine said regretfully, "If it didn't have that bit of my finger in the corner, it would be even better. I was so excited at having something really exciting to shoot that I forgot how to handle the camera."

Myrtle pulled the picture aside and put it on the end table next to her chair. She slowly cycled through the rest of the pictures. There were quite a few of Jack that she thought were absolutely darling but probably weren't exactly photographic masterpieces. There were a few of downtown Bradley with close-ups of the old Coca Cola sign on Bo's Diner. Pictures of the American flags flanking the tree-lined main street. And then there were some midrange shots of gatherings. Some old ladies gossiping at the farmer's market, some old men cutting up outside the gas station.

And—there was another shot of Cousin Charles. This time he wasn't fighting but appeared to be having a deep and meaningful conversation with Myrtle's dentist. She spotted that red hair right off the bat. She frowned. Did Cousin Charles have bad teeth? Why was he being so serious?

"So—what do you think?" asked Elaine, looking anxious.

"I think Cousin Charles was a troublemaker," said Myrtle with conviction.

"I mean...what do you think about the pictures? Do I have any talent, do you think? And—who's Cousin Charles? Don't tell me you have even more relatives." It seemed as though having potentially more Clover in-laws made Elaine uncomfortable.

"I think your pictures are very interesting," said Myrtle truthfully. "Particularly the subject matter. Yes, I think you have a real knack for composition."

Elaine breathed out. "Good. Because, I wanted to ask Red for a better camera. He said he didn't want to shell out a bunch of money unless it looked like I might stick with this hobby."

Unlike her other hobbies.

"Cousin Charles, since you asked, is the victim. Didn't I mention that? He's not my cousin—he's Miles's. And you've got two pictures of him," said Myrtle.

"Really? That's great! When I show Red, maybe it'll bring him on-board with my photography. You know how he always regards my hobbies with suspicion," said Elaine.

And rightfully so. "Do you mind if I make a copy of these pictures before you show Red? For my own records?" asked Myrtle.

Elaine looked puzzled, then smiled. "Oh, I see. You're investigating again."

"I've got to clear Miles's name, of course. Miles has been a good friend," said Myrtle nobly.

"Does Red know? He gets pretty upset when you start nosing around his cases," said Elaine.

"I didn't mention my plans to him, no. If you could keep it on the down-low, I'd appreciate it, Elaine. It's none of Red's business, anyway," said Myrtle.

Elaine grinned at her. "Technically, as police chief, it *is* his business. But don't worry, I won't say anything." She copied the pictures on her printer and handed them to Myrtle.

"You know, Elaine, I bet Sloan Jones could use a freelance photographer for the paper. Maybe you can help him out by snapping some pictures and sending them over," said Myrtle.

"Do you really think so?" asked Elaine, squinting doubtfully. "Are they that good?"

Unfortunately, they weren't. But it was a small town. "You'll only get better, Elaine. And think about it—you're frequently out and about with Jack, so you're practically designed to be a photo correspondent. I'll mention it to Sloan." Myrtle had a helpful hints column in the paper. It was the kind of paper that was heavy on gossip, crosswords, astrology, and want ads.

"I'm not sure," said Elaine, watching Jack now crashing the cars into each other in what was probably a cry for help before he ended up taking a nap. "What kinds of pictures do you think Sloan needs?"

"You know the kinds of stories the *Bradley Bugle* focuses on. A human interest piece on Mrs. Flotman's prize-winning tomatoes. The new hot dog shop opening up downtown. An Eagle Scout ceremony. The Bradley High School football game. The types of migrating birds at your bird feeder. So-and-so's new baby. You'll be perfect," said Myrtle. "And maybe you'll even end up taking some more pictures that tie into this case."

Elaine chuckled. "I see. So you're wanting to review these pictures."

Myrtle shrugged. "Maybe I can even give you some tips. Not that I know much about photography, but maybe I can think of some places for you to go to get different types of shots." She said thoughtfully, "Like Cousin Charles's funeral."

"Myrtle! I can't just go around taking pictures at a private funeral. Sloan doesn't put that kind of stuff in the newspaper—it would be an invasion of privacy. And grief."

"I'm not saying that anyone has to actually see you taking them, Elaine. Maybe you can just use your zoom lens and take some from inside your car. We can study them later on. It could be good practice, taking long distance shots," said Myrtle.

"Maybe. When is the funeral?"

Myrtle said, "I'm not exactly sure. I guess they'll have to do an autopsy on the body first before they release him to the family. I'd think it would be a few days away." She paused. "I'm going to be giving the reception for the family after the funeral."

Elaine's eyes opened wide. "You are? At your house?"

"I thought it would be a good idea. Who knows—maybe Charles's killer will be in attendance and I can pick up some clues," said Myrtle.

"You're planning on serving food?" Elaine's voice sounded strained.

Myrtle gave a frustrated sigh. "Why does everyone keep asking me that? Of course I'm serving food. It's a Southern funeral. People will be expecting ham biscuits, cucumber sandwiches, pimento cheese, and fried chicken. They'll want to feel *comforted*, for heaven's sake."

Elaine gave a quick nod, looking away. "Well, let me know when they set a date and time and I'll come. I'm happy to bring some food, too, to help you out."

"Thanks." Myrtle leaned on her cane and stood up. "I probably should be getting home now. If I'm going to be hosting this thing, I need to call Dusty and Puddin and convince them to come back. Knowing those two, they probably consider themselves done for the week." She peered out Elaine's front window.

"Is the coast clear?" asked Elaine dryly.

"No signs of Erma Sherman, although that doesn't mean she's not spying on your house and waiting for me to walk out your door. Nosy woman," said Myrtle in irritation.

If Elaine thought that was the pot calling the kettle black, she wisely gave no indication of it.

Chapter Four

U nfortunately, Erma *was* lying in wait for her. She must have had that long nose of hers pressed up against the window, watching for Myrtle to come out. Myrtle's cane was only halfway out Elaine's door when Erma came galloping out of her house. Myrtle groaned.

For years, she'd come up with a range of polite excuses to be on her way instead of engaging in conversation with her next-door neighbor. She'd say that she had a pot boiling or that she was expecting an important phone call. Erma was one of those rare people who were completely oblivious to polite excuses. She kept right on bulldozing through a monologue of the confusing dream she'd had the night before or the rash she couldn't seem to get rid of. Erma wasn't the type who even picked up on rudeness.

"Myrtle!" said Erma, grabbing her arm and pulling her along to her house. "Come with me and sit down for a while. You must be in shock from finding a body in your backyard. I was in shock one time. It does funny things to you. Makes you feel like you can't breathe, makes your chest hurt. Makes you go numb...."

"Aren't those the symptoms of a heart attack?" asked Myrtle irritably. "If you're feeling any of those now, you should get over to the emergency room."

"No, this was from a long time ago. When I won the sweepstakes. Not the really *big* prize, but it was a lot of money. A lot! And I was in shock, that's what the doctor said."

Myrtle pulled her arm away. "I can't talk now, Erma—I've got to make some phone calls. To Puddin and Dusty, for one."

"Those two! I don't know why you put up with them." Erma gawked in horror at Myrtle's yard, which admittedly did look pretty horrible with the half-mowed grass and the weeds sticking up around all the gnomes' heels. "If my yard looked like that, then I'd be firing my yardman right away. And Puddin...." Her voice trailed off as she became uncharacteristically speechless.

Myrtle said, "Yes, well, if I got rid of them I wouldn't be able to find anyone else, would I? You know how Bradley is. The only other yard-man around here is so booked up that he can only mow every other week at all of his customer's houses. Same with the housekeepers—all the good ones are booked solid. Puddin is a disgrace, but at least she's available to work." Most of the time.

"Whatever. What I really wanted to tell you, Myrtle, is that I know who is behind this! I was awake last night around ten or eleven and kept hearing noises and seeing things. That awful cat of yours was making so much racket that I turned on my oscillating fan to drown out the sound so I could sleep. Now that I know about the murder, though, everything is clear to me." Erma smirked at Myrtle in a secretive, smug way.

"Who's the killer then, Erma? Who did it?" asked Myrtle.

Erma leaned close enough into Myrtle that she could smell the onions on her breath. She whispered, "It was Miles. I know it for a fact. Miles killed the man in your backyard. You should watch out for him—he's a very dangerous man. He lives close. The victim was related to him and reportedly wanted his money. And Pasha hates him. Yes, it was Miles. He's a killer."

Myrtle snorted. "I'll take that under advisement, Erma." She walked away from her as quickly as she could, cane thumping on the ground as she went.

"It's true," she yodeled from behind Myrtle. "I have clues! And I'm telling Red about them!"

"You do that," hollered Myrtle as she hurried away. Madness. She was always surrounded by complete and utter madness.

She closed the door behind her and locked it—*not* because Red had told her to, but because she was scared spitless that crazy Erma Sherman would come barreling through the door to tell her all her clues and theories about Miles being a killer. Miles. On the bright side, though, if she blabbed coyly to enough people that she knew who the murderer was and that she had clues, then *she, herself* might end up as a body in the backyard.

Myrtle walked to her small desk and pulled out a notebook and pencil. She was going to need to talk to suspects and she needed to ascertain whom these suspects might be. She tapped the pencil against the notebook. There was Lee Woosley, for one...the guy who'd been fighting with Charles at a poker game just the other night. Could he have killed him out of rage? But why would he have followed him over to Myrtle's house to kill him?

And there was Hugh Bass—Myrtle's dentist. Elaine's picture of Charles and Hugh together had been pretty interesting. Dr. Bass wasn't a particularly grim man, but he'd sure looked serious in that picture. Charles's face had been telling, too—he had a very knowing expression. There'd also been a touch of unholy glee present on his features.

So she definitely wanted to talk to those two. And neither one sounded particularly likely to go to the funeral to pay his respects. Myrtle reached out for the phone.

"Yes, I'd like to make an appointment please, Pam. For a cleaning, if I could. I'm sure I'm probably due for one. What? That long ago? Tomorrow morning will be fine, if you can fit me in. This is with Dr. Bass, right? I don't want to see anyone else. You still don't have any other doctors in the practice, right? Okay, thanks." At least she could have a chance to talk to Dr. Bass by himself. If she could get rid of the hygienist, that is.

Lee Woosley. Hmm. Well, she wasn't prepared to start playing poker in order to hang out with Lee for a while. What on earth did the man do for a living? She tapped the pencil against the paper as she thought. Didn't he do repairs of some kind? That's right—he was a handyman. She glanced around her living room. There had to be something that needed to be repaired around here. The problem was that Red was always messing in her business and popping over with his toolbox to fix things. But that meant that he'd know what still needed fixing.

She hesitated, then picked up the phone again.

Red answered, sounding hurried. There were voices in the background that had an official edge to them. "Mama? Hey, what's going on? I've got the state police here, talking over the case."

"In your tiny office? Shouldn't y'all meet out somewhere or something?" asked Myrtle.

"It's not exactly a conversation to have at the ice cream parlor, Mama. Or Bo's Diner. What's up?"

"Do you know, offhand, what kinds of repairs I need to make to my house? You know—the honey-do type stuff?" asked Myrtle.

"Why do you have to know this right now? I've been asking you to take care of that stuff for ages or to make me a list so that I could help you with it. Is there a problem at your house?" Myrtle could tell by his voice that he was getting worked up. He always thought her house was some kind of deathtrap. If he had his way, she'd have been at Greener Pastures retirement home for the last couple of decades.

"No, no problem. I'm just trying to be proactive," said Myrtle.

Now Red sounded suspicious. "Proactive? About repairs in your house? This *is* Myrtle Clover that I'm on the phone with, right?"

"Don't be so sassy, Red. Now think. What repairs are needed at my house that you know of?"

"There's the towel rack in the hall bathroom for one—it's coming off the wall."

"Okay," said Myrtle, jotting that down on her notepad.

"And your tub needs to be caulked," said Red.

"All right."

"Your garbage disposal doesn't really work—I think it may need replacing," said Red.

"Hmm."

"The light in your closet has some sort of short or something in it that needs to be checked out. I don't want you stumbling in your closet in the dark," said Red.

"Fine," said Myrtle in a tight voice, starting to feel irritated.

"The planter on the back wall of your house pulled off the wall and needs to be put back up," said Red helpfully.

"I think that's probably enough."

"A grab bar in your tub would be very useful, Mama. And I don't really know where to get started with your dock. One day it's just going to come loose from its moorings and start floating away on the lake with the boat still attached."

Myrtle fumed, tapping the pencil on the paper again.

"The toilet paper holder in the hall bath is also trying to come off the wall," said Red. "Oh, and you could use a door stop on your backdoor—your backdoor keeps hitting your kitchen counter whenever it swings open too far."

"Enough!" said Myrtle. This would cost her a mint. "Good luck with your case," she said and hung up. For heaven's sake.

Myrtle walked back over to her desk and woke up her computer. She typed in Lee Woosley's name into the local business listing page and pulled up his phone number.

"Lee?" she said, minutes later. "This is Myrtle Clover."

"Mrs. Clover?" Lee had apparently been napping and her name was enough to startle him out of his sleep. "Wow, I haven't talked to you since English class about thirty years ago."

"Yes. Well. Hope you're doing well." Myrtle was a retired English teacher and was used to former students being bumfuddled in her presence. "Listen, I was hoping you could help me out with some projects I need to get taken care of around my house."

"Oh, I see. You have some home repair projects that you need help with," said Lee, sounding relieved.

"That's right."

Lee laughed ruefully. "I kind of had a flashback there for a moment. Thought you were going to ask me to come in for extra tutoring in English or something. You know how that wasn't my subject."

Had he *had* a subject he was good at? Myrtle doubted it.

"Want me to come out tomorrow?" asked Lee.

Myrtle started to agree, but remembered she'd just set up that dental appointment for the next day. Since she hadn't made it over there for a while, who knew how long it would take? "Maybe the next day will be better, Lee."

"What kind of stuff do you need done, Mrs. Clover?" asked Lee.

She glanced at the list she'd made from the talk with Red. There was no way she was going to get him to do all these things when she really just wanted to talk to him about Charles. "Nothing too exciting. I have a towel rack and a toilet paper holder that are pulling away from the wall and a tub that needs caulking," said Myrtle. "Oh and there's a planter that I'd really like hung back up to the side of my house. It pulled off and I can't get it to stay back on."

They arranged a time for a couple of days out and Myrtle hung up, feeling pleased with herself. This was coming along nicely. At this rate, she'd know who the killer was before Red had even started questioning suspects.

After all the excitement of a body in the yard and all the activity that followed it, Myrtle decided to put her feet up for a little while. Most of the time she really didn't feel her eighty-odd years, but when she *did* it was always her feet that gave her away.

Her insomnia from the night before had apparently had more of an impact on her than she thought. A few minutes after she'd started her recording of her soap opera, *Tomorrow's Promise*, she dropped off to sleep. Later, this would irritate her because she wouldn't know where exactly she'd left off and would need to find the spot.

The sound of her doorbell usually would make her jump into life but this time the sound didn't jar her into awareness because she thought she must be hearing it on the television. By the time she realized it actually was her own doorbell, her caller had taken to rapping on the door. "Coming!" she called loudly, reaching down to fumble for her cane. The cane developed a mind of its own and scooted away from Myrtle under the coffee table. "Shoot! Hold your horses, I'm coming!"

She finally got to the door and peeped out to make sure there wasn't a maniacal killer on her doorstep. It was only Sloan Jones, her editor at the local newspaper and another former student of hers. He was ordinarily a little intimidated by his former teacher but had lately gotten more comfortable in Myrtle's presence.

Her irritation at the past minute of scrambling must have showed on her face, though. "Uh oh. Did I wake you up, Miss Myrtle?" His big face with its ever-expanding forehead was anxious. "Sorry."

"It's okay," said Myrtle, motioning him in and closing the door behind her. "I hadn't planned on falling asleep anyway. I've got things to do."

She sat down on the sofa, but Sloan walked straight through her living room and kitchen to peer out her back window into the backyard. He had his camera with him. "Miss Myrtle," he said, squinting through his viewfinder and lining up a shot through the window. "Is it okay if I take a few pictures from inside your kitchen and right outside your back door? Of the tragic scene—you know."

"To put in the paper? Isn't that sort of morbid for the *Bradley Bugle*, Sloan? We're talking about the kind of newspaper that reports the number of Girl Scout cookies sold by the local troop as a major news story," said Myrtle.

He turned to look at her. "No, I won't run the picture. That's too lurid for us. But I want to be able to accurately describe the scene for my story. It helps me out if I look at a picture while I'm writing it." He looked back through the viewfinder and took a couple more shots.

"*Your* story?" Myrtle frowned. "No, this is my story."

Sloan turned around again. "Red told me you didn't need to have any more crime stories to work on, Miss Myrtle. He's worried you're going to get hurt. You're supposed to just write your helpful hints column and maybe fill in as a writer for some of the other columns if somebody goes on vacation."

"Pooh on Red! Sloan, he has no business getting involved in my affairs. No business at all. You're the editor of the newspaper. Actually, you're the *publisher* of the paper. What you say goes. You know I do an excellent job with all the stories I write for the paper—especially those crime stories."

Sloan shifted his weight uncomfortably. "The problem, Miss Myrtle, is that it's important that I have a good working relationship with Red—with him being the police chief and all. Sometimes he'll give me information for stories...you know."

Myrtle did know. And she didn't like it.

"That might well be. But I've got the inside scoop, Sloan, and I'm going to keep it to myself unless you give me this story. The body was in my backyard after all, and I had a front row seat for all the investigating. I also have a source with some pictures of the victim in the days preceding his death," said Myrtle. Never let it be said that she was a pushover. If you wanted something badly enough, you needed to go for it.

Sloan thoughtfully rubbed his balding head. "Well...okay. I guess it makes sense for you to cover it. I might run a short story on the blog, though, to report on the murder until we get the print edition out. You don't need to investigate the murder, though. All I need for you to do is to write up the story as it unfolds—I don't need you to solve the thing." He followed Myrtle back into her living room and they sat down on her sofa.

"Naturally," said Myrtle. "I wouldn't dream of doing such a thing!" Sloan looked vastly relieved. It was interesting how gullible a newspaperman could be.

"I'm going to cover it from a human interest standpoint, too," said Myrtle. "I'll talk to some of the people who knew him and get some reactions to his death. Murder is so rare here that everyone is probably in shock and would like to talk it out."

Sloan said, "Actually, the murder rate in our little hamlet is astonishingly high, Miss Myrtle. I can't for the life of me figure it out." He shook his head, then looked at her closer. "A source? You said you had a source with pictures of the victim before he passed?"

"That's right. Oh, I don't know if we need to publish those pictures or anything, but it's nice to have them available. Did you know anything about the victim, by any chance? I don't think he was in town for very long before he died," said Myrtle. "I'd like to talk to anybody who might have a connection with him. Just for the human interest side of the piece," she added in a hurry since Sloan looked suspicious again. He clearly didn't need to know that she was going to be investigating.

"As a matter of fact, I did see the guy around town. Not that I really knew who he was at the time, but you know how new people stand out. Although he did grow up here, so I guess he wasn't all that new," said Sloan.

Sloan was fond of hanging out at the local tavern after work and was likely to have run across Charles more than most people. "Did you have a chance to talk to him? What was he like?"

"He was a pain in the rear end," said Sloan in a rueful voice. "When I saw him he was either arguing over cards or being a real ugly drunk. And then there's his little dalliance with Annette Dawson." He raised his eyebrows at Myrtle.

"A dalliance? I thought the man had just gotten into town. He must move fast," said Myrtle.

"I don't think he'd *just* moved into town, no. I think he'd been here a couple of weeks."

"That seems pretty recent to me," said Myrtle, having been in Bradley for over eighty years.

"I saw him one night when I was at the tavern. Annette Dawson was sitting real close to him at the bar and laughing at every little thing he said. She was still wearing her scrubs from her shift at the county hospital, so I guess that's why she was out that late," said Sloan.

Myrtle frowned. "But Annette Dawson is married. She's been married to Silas Dawson for ages, hasn't she?"

"Pretty much. For about twenty years, I'd say. She's a lot older than Charles, too. But she's still real nice looking." Sloan looked wistful. His love life had consisted of scattered and unsuccessful dating and a long period where he lived with his mother before the newspaper started showing a modest profit.

Myrtle was thoughtful. "Silas doesn't strike me as the kind of man who would let his wife carry on a flagrant affair with another man."

"He's a tough guy," said Sloan with a shiver. "He's real wiry and strong. He wasn't happy to find his wife with another man."

"So he *did* find out?"

"Of course he did, Miss Myrtle. This is Bradley, after all. He found out just days later. I was at the tavern when he came in to take Annette back home with him. He took Charles by surprise and punched him right in the gut." Sloan put a protective hand over his own substantial gut. "He couldn't talk or anything. While he was trying to get his breath back, Silas gave him a real piece of his mind and told him to stay away from his wife."

"I wonder if Silas could have murdered Charles," said Myrtle. "He must have been furious at being made a fool of."

"Lots of people are talking about it," said Sloan.

"Do you think Red knows about it?" asked Myrtle.

"Well, the fight wasn't reported to the police, so he didn't find out about it that way. It wasn't really much of a fight, since it was just a single blow. Besides, Bill—that's the bartender—he felt sorry for Silas and thought Charles got what was coming to him...so he didn't call Red. Red might have heard some of the gossip, though." Sloan gave Myrtle a reproachful look. "I'm giving you all these juicy details and you're not telling me anything about what happened here this morning."

And she wasn't going to tell him much, that's for sure. It was her story, after all. "Well, Dusty and Puddin were here, doing yard work and cleaning the house."

"Were they?" Sloan stared doubtfully at the dust on the end table next to the sofa.

"They didn't finish doing the yard or cleaning the house because of the body," said Myrtle with a sigh. "I've got to call them and get them both back over. I'm having the family reception after the funeral."

"Are you?" Sloan looked startled. "You're serving food?"

Myrtle scowled at him. "What is wrong with everyone? Yes, of course I'm serving food! I swear to goodness, we need to have some more deaths here in Bradley. There's a serious lack of education when it comes to funeral protocol here."

"Sorry," said Sloan. He covered up his mouth and Myrtle was suspicious that he might be smiling for some reason. "Go on with your story please, Miss Myrtle. You were saying that Puddin and Dusty were here."

"Yes. Dusty discovered the body and left to get Red, Puddin started screaming, and Miles came over to identify the victim as his cousin," said Myrtle.

"I thought I heard that the man was killed by one of your gnomes," said Sloan, again with some unidentified emotion tugging his lips into odd shapes.

"That's right. He was hit over the head with my Viking gnome. It was very vexing to me, too," said Myrtle, still fuming over the thought of her favorite gnome being used as a weapon...and getting broken. "The police ended up taking it away to analyze it."

She swore he was trying to stifle a laugh. "That must be very traumatic for you," he said in a muffled voice.

"Hmm. Well, it was," she said. After a moment, she said, "By the way, I wanted to let you know that my daughter-in-law is now doing photography. She has—some very *interesting* photos that she's taken around town. Elaine and I thought there was a possibility that you might like some pictures sometimes and she's out in Bradley enough that she'll likely have plenty. Just to let you know," said Myrtle.

Sloan said, "If she wants to act as a freelance photographer, then I'm sure I'll be interested in buying some of her pictures from time to time. I can't hire anybody else on staff, though. If she wants to upload pictures to the blog, that might be the best idea. That way if she has a great picture of downtown Bradley with kids selling lemonade on the corner, she can put it up on the blog and that gives me easy content. Folks always comment on that kind of stuff, too. 'Bradley is the best town ever! I feel like I've stepped back into the 1950s!' That kind of thing."

"I'll let her know, then," said Myrtle. If Sloan knew the kind of photographer he was dealing with, he'd want to preview those pictures before they went up on the blog. He's going to end up with lots of pictures of Elaine's finger or blurry pictures of unidentifiable objects.

Chapter Five

Myrtle could tell it was going to be one of those nights where she couldn't sleep. As soon as she lay down, her mind became fixated on things she needed to do to prepare for the little reception after the funeral. She'd tell herself to relax, take deep breaths, gradually stretch her muscles and feel that she was about to drift off...and some other detail would pop into her head and mess it all up again.

When she finally did fall asleep, her dreams were of that weird, am-I-awake-or-am-I-asleep, quality that played with her head. She kept glancing at her clock, convinced it must almost be morning but saw instead that it was only fifteen or twenty minutes later from the last time she'd checked. Finally, she gave a frustrated bellow, untangled herself from the tangled bed sheets, and propelled herself out of the bed.

It was two o'clock in the morning. This was her usual time for being awake and it wasn't that she was unprepared for it. Ordinarily, she'd putter around the house—start a load of laundry, put away the dishes from the dishwasher, read a few chapters of a book. Sometimes she'd take a walk down the street. Her neighbors had grown accustomed to seeing a tall, white-headed person in a bathrobe navigating down the sidewalk in the middle of the night. Unfortunately, Red, if he were the one to see her, never missed the opportunity to remind her that Greener Pastures retirement home was an excellent, safe place for wandering octogenarians.

The thought of Red made Myrtle settle docilely in her armchair and turn on the TV for the rest of her *Tomorrow's Promise* soap opera that she'd fallen asleep during earlier. Five minutes into the show, though, she became uncharacteristically annoyed by it. Melaina was in the hospital *again*? That woman had been in the hospital the past few months with every illness known to man—cancer, rehab, a car crash, a gunshot wound. Couldn't the writers come up with something new for her to do?

Myrtle turned off the TV, feeling restless again. Sleep wasn't going to happen, so she might as well stretch her legs. Red should be sleeping soundly after all the excitement of the murder. She brightened. Maybe Miles would be awake. He frequently had insomnia himself. She put on her robe, pulled out a bag of cookies and hung them from a plastic bag on her wrist, grabbed her cane, and headed outside the door. She even remembered to lock the door behind her.

Myrtle wandered down the sidewalk, then peered at Miles's house. There were lights on, all right. They didn't look like nightlights, either. Myrtle walked up his front walk and rang Miles's doorbell.

Miles answered the door. "I figured you might come over. I set the coffeemaker to perk at one-thirty."

Myrtle grinned at him, delighted to have someone to talk to in the middle of the night. "I'm late, then! Let's get started. I brought some gingersnaps."

Miles smiled back at her. Minutes later, they munched on cookies and drank milk and coffee. Myrtle said thoughtfully, "You didn't set an alarm for yourself or anything did you? Because you thought I might come over?"

"Nothing like that. I just anticipated that you might have insomnia tonight—I know your mind starts getting real active when you have a new case to mull over," said Miles.

Myrtle gave a satisfied sigh. "I like the way you put that, Miles. A case. That's what I've got. A new puzzle to solve."

"Although more dangerous than any of your crossword puzzles," said Miles. "You weren't worried about walking over here in the dark? You did have a murder right in your own backyard last night, after all."

Myrtle shrugged. "It had nothing to do with me, did it? Seems like it had more to do with you. I'm only trying to get to the bottom of it, that's all. Why would someone want to kill me?"

Miles wisely bit his tongue. Myrtle looked suspiciously at him.

Miles quickly said, "So what, in particular, is on your mind, Myrtle? What kept you up tonight?"

"Oh, I was mulling it all over. I was also planning the reception in my head," said Myrtle.

Miles looked blankly at her.

"For heaven's sake, Miles! You haven't already forgotten, have you? The family reception that I'm having for you and your loved ones! At my house! After the funeral!"

"My loved ones?" Miles chuckled. "I wouldn't call them that, actually. We'll just leave it at family. Yes, I remember all about it now...thanks."

"Were family members calling you up yesterday afternoon and trying to get information from you about the funeral plans?" asked Myrtle.

"No, they weren't. I really don't know who even knows or particularly cares about Cousin Charles's death. He was a black sheep, after all. I can't imagine that I'm the only one who isn't interested in claiming him."

Myrtle said, "What about your aunt? Surely you've talked to her."

Miles sighed. "I have. She's distraught in sort of a melodramatic and possibly not very genuine way. She said that the police told her that she would be able to have the funeral four days from now. So...if you're determined to host people at your house...I guess you can plan it for then. Although I'm still baffled why you'd want to."

"Mostly I'm trying to look for suspect reactions," said Myrtle.

Miles raised his eyebrows. "Do you know who the suspects even are?"

"Not really. That's another reason why I want these people over. It'll give me a chance to look at them, listen to them, and figure out their connection to your cousin. Maybe it'll even give me the opportunity to learn which of them might have wanted to do away with him," said Myrtle. She frowned thoughtfully. "Although, it sounds as if your family may not be cooperative. So I'll make it an open invitation to anyone who attends the funeral service."

"Are you sure you want to do that? What if a bunch of people end up showing up at your house? You don't have a whole lot of room, you know," said Miles.

"Then they can just go spilling out into the yard," said Myrtle with a shrug. "I'm not worried. It's not like they're sleeping there or anything. I can handle anything for a couple of hours. Speaking of my yard, I was thinking about putting a sort of makeshift memorial in my yard." As Miles squinted at her in confusion, Myrtle irritably explained, "You know. To mark the spot where Charles met his Maker." Miles kept squinting at her. "People do that! I see it all the time."

"What...like a bunch of pink and blue teddy bears with balloons and roses?" Miles's voice was very doubtful. "That doesn't sound like Cousin Charles."

"Oh. Okay. Maybe a simple vase of roses?" Myrtle asked.

Miles shook his head.

"A white cross? It could be discreet."

Miles squinted. "I can't see Cousin Charles as a particularly devout man."

"A small American flag?"

"He wasn't a veteran," said Miles. "The military was way too smart to enlist Charles."

"For heaven's sake! How about a whiskey bottle and a glass then?" said Myrtle in exasperation.

"Hmm," said Miles as if seriously considering her suggestion. "Sort of like the bottle of cognac the mysterious visitor would leave at Poe's grave?" He saw her frowning at him and said, "I know what you mean. I just can't think of a way of doing something like that without it being super-campy. Besides, any memorial you put out might be hard to see with your grass as tall as it is. Why do you want to have one?"

"I thought that I might catch someone looking morosely out the window at the little memorial. Regretting what they'd done, lamenting the state of violence in this world that influenced them to such a horrid act. That sort of thing," Myrtle finished vaguely.

"Aren't they more likely to be looking out the window in a very satisfied manner?" asked Miles, carefully breaking off a piece of a gingersnap. "Admiring their handiwork? Proud of their accomplishment?"

"That's a fairly cynical way of looking at it," said Myrtle, annoyed that she hadn't broadened her imaginings of what a murderer might feel.

"Remember what we're dealing with—Cousin Charles. He wasn't the finest example of humanity ever to walk the planet, regardless of what my aunt might think. In fact, a murderer might even feel quite noble about ridding the world of Charles...who knows?" said Miles.

"Who indeed?" muttered Myrtle. "I think I'll plan on something small and tasteful to mark the spot, then." Although she had no idea what that would be.

"I think that Sloan is running an obituary in the paper tomorrow with some of the funeral arrangements listed. Should I get him to add a small sentence about your reception?" asked Miles.

"Why not? When is it running? Tomorrow-tomorrow, or today-tomorrow? Since it's two a.m. now, you're not saying it's running this morning, right? I don't think we should pull poor Sloan out of his bed to add to the obituary," said Myrtle.

"No, *tomorrow*-tomorrow. So it'll run in another twenty-four hours. Plenty of time to add it. I'll call him later today," said Miles.

Myrtle said, "By the way, Sloan assigned me the story. The murder. He said that I could write it for the paper." She was worried about Miles's reaction to this news. Sometimes he'd start acting very cold and she didn't understand why. Myrtle hoped this wasn't going to be one of those times.

Miles nodded and didn't appear to change his mood, which was a relief. "I figured you might get that story, considering it happened literally in your backyard." He paused. "This doesn't mean you're going to pester me for quotes, does it?" The coldness was now trickling in a little.

"Maybe just a very general one, Miles," said Myrtle. "Nothing extremely personal. Just a statement of who he was and how you were related."

Miles considered this. "No. No, I don't think I want my connection with Charles in the paper. It's enough for me to go to the funeral and deal with my aunt and go to the reception and talk to the police. If I can prevent more people from knowing that the two of us were related, that works for me."

Myrtle just blinked at him. "Well, that's most disappointing, Miles!" She took a sip of her milk while she thought over the implications of this unexpected complication. "Although I suppose it won't make a huge difference to the story, since your quote was going to be such a minor one, anyway." She frowned. "But you're still going to help me with my investigating, aren't you? You'll still be my sidekick?"

Miles grinned at her. "So you admit that I *am* a sidekick? In the past, you've downplayed my role in your cases. Pooh-poohed my contributions."

"I've done no such thing. Naturally, you're a sidekick. For heaven's sake. You have a car, and everything! You're still driving, too," said Myrtle.

"Oh, *now* I know my desirability as a sidekick. I've got wheels and a driver's license."

"Don't be silly. I have a driver's license, myself. But I don't have a car anymore," said Myrtle. Reluctantly she added, "And you contribute more than just transportation. I like bouncing ideas off, too." She was still waiting to hear what he had to say about getting involved in the investigation.

Miles said, "I have the feeling that even if I say I want nothing to do with this case, which I'm sorely tempted to do, that I'll somehow get dragged into it against my will. Since being dragged into things usually irritates me, I'll go ahead and plan on being involved." Myrtle clapped her hands and he quickly added, "But I'm getting involved *not* as a relative of this person. I want to treat this as an ordinary case where we work on the side of justice to subvert evil in Bradley, North Carolina." Myrtle looked closely at him to see whether he was being facetious. It wasn't like Miles to speak in such grandiose terms.

"How about solving it because you're clearing your name?" suggested Myrtle. "Considering how you are a suspect in the case." He glowered at her and she said, "All right! All right! I'll presume you're completely innocent while investigating the murder."

"Thanks," said Miles. She thought she detected a touch of sarcasm in his voice.

They munched silently on the cookies for a minute or two. "So," said Miles finally, "since I'm your sidekick, why don't you share some of your investigation with me? Who are you considering as suspects?"

"First of all, I'm putting Lee Woosley on my suspect list," said Myrtle.

"Of course—the man who was fighting with Charles at the poker game," said Miles, nodding. "That makes sense. Good thing that Red mentioned that he'd broken up that fight or we wouldn't even have one name on the list."

"Actually, I don't even need Red anymore," said Myrtle with a sniff. "I have Elaine."

"Elaine? Myrtle, you're not sticking Elaine in the middle of all this, are you? Putting her in the middle between you and Red on a case? She can't win!" said Miles.

"No, it's nothing like that. Elaine has a new hobby," said Myrtle.

Miles's eyes widened in alarm behind his steel-rimmed glasses. He'd been right there beside Myrtle through Elaine's other hobbies. None of them had ended particularly well and usually entailed his home being the repository for various bits of Elaine's pottery or other malformed artwork.

"Don't worry," said Myrtle. "It's not as bad as it usually is. This time it's photography."

Miles relaxed in the kitchen chair. "It's hard to mess that up."

"Well, don't underestimate Elaine. I think we have some blurry images in store. And lots of photos of her various fingers. Not to mention pictures that should have had the flash turned on."

Miles groaned.

"But I will say this for her—she has a knack for being in the right place at the right time. She took a picture of the exciting fight that Red broke up...she was with Red at the time that he got the call and was practicing action shots. She also took a fascinating picture of Hugh Bass having a very serious conversation with your cousin," said Myrtle.

"Hugh Bass? Isn't he a dentist here in town?"

Myrtle said, "He's *everyone's* dentist. Bradley is a very small town."

"How on earth could he have known Charles?" Miles frowned. "That's rather disturbing. I don't think I'll let him put his hands on my teeth."

Miles's teeth were apparently a source of pride to him. She supposed that anyone who made it to seventy with all their teeth in perfect condition would feel that way. Myrtle wouldn't know.

"I don't know how he knows him, but I'm going to find out. I'm going to the dentist tomorrow to have my teeth cleaned and I'm prepared to ask questions," said Myrtle.

"How are you going to do that? Whenever I go to the dentist, I can't get a word in edgewise because someone's hands are always in my mouth."

Myrtle said, "Oh, I have my ways. People can be extremely deferential when it comes to old, frail, garrulous ladies. I'll let you know everything I find out." She looked at Miles's wall clock. "I wish I were feeling sleepy, but I'm not. Did you watch *Tomorrow's Promise* this afternoon?"

Miles was still somewhat chagrined that he was hooked on the show, but he clearly wanted to talk about it. "I only got as far as Melaina being admitted to the hospital again."

Myrtle clapped her hands. "That's where I left off, too!"

"I'll start up the tape."

Chapter Six

The town of Bradley had been very pleased to have Dr. Bass move back to town, Myrtle remembered, as she walked the short distance down the dogwood-lined street to the downtown office the next day.

The previous dentist had been Dr. Bissell. He'd been as old as Myrtle and determined not to retire. He'd been taking care of the dental needs for the town since Myrtle had been in her early twenties. One day, he'd taken his usual lunchtime nap in the office (the office always closed for lunch between the hours of twelve and one) and hadn't woken up. It had shocked Pam the hygienist to pieces and she'd taken to her bed for well-nigh on to a month.

Luckily, considering that Bradley was a town that enjoyed sweets, one of its own had returned to town to take over the small practice. Dr. Bass had grown up in Bradley and was happy to step in. He even kept Pam as hygienist, and persuaded her that she had recuperated from her shock by that point. For the past five years, Dr. Bass had ministered to the Bradley citizen's teeth with few complaints from the populace. Except that sometimes there was a long wait.

This was a morning that involved waiting. Myrtle sighed. It was probably because they'd worked her into their schedule, but she'd already been there for twenty minutes with absolutely no sign of being taken back. She looked morosely around the waiting room. Same vinyl chairs mixed in with high-backed wooden chairs. There were a few anemic-looking plants that appeared to be in desperate need of water. Myrtle reached for a magazine. It was a magazine on healthy living that was months old. She made a face and put it back. The others were just as uninteresting: one on motorbikes, a gardening magazine, an RV magazine, and one on camping. Bleh.

She never thought she'd be so relieved to be called back to the dentist. Of course, she had to see Pam, the hygienist, first. She'd forgotten that Pam would actually clean her teeth. Myrtle sighed.

Pam was too cheerful, Myrtle thought. And she had that irritating habit of calling everyone over the age of sixty *sweetheart* and other pet names. She wasn't Pam's sweetheart or pet. She wasn't anyone's sweetheart and she wasn't cute or darling. And never had been.

This went on for some time while Myrtle gritted the teeth that Pam was trying to clean.

Pam simpered, "Darlin', you need to relax just a little bit. It's too hard for me to clean these pretty teeth of yours."

Myrtle frowned at her, a realization dawning. "Didn't I teach you?" asked Myrtle. "A *long* time ago? Thirty-five years ago, maybe?"

Pam's bright smile faltered and her voice got tighter, "Yes ma'am, I believe you might have."

Funny how quickly a *darlin'* changed into a *ma'am*.

Dr. Bass was apparently wildly busy. Myrtle could hear him in another room, checking the teeth of another patient. Then she heard him in the room next door. Finally, he stuck his head into her room. Pam, however, wasn't quite done with the cleaning. This was probably due to Myrtle's clenched teeth earlier, which had delayed the process.

The dentist came over to politely say hello. He looked to be in his mid-thirties with a thick head of red hair. "Hi, Mrs. Clover. I see you're not done yet, so I'm going to run over and check another patient and come right back."

Myrtle tried to say something, but Pam stuck one of those sucking instruments in her mouth and she had to hurry to get her tongue out of the way. Pam blinked innocently at Myrtle, but she swore she saw a trace of vindictiveness there. Myrtle had one-upped her in their little verbal volley.

Myrtle quickly became more compliant a patient in the hopes that Pam would finally finish the cleaning, and she could have that conversation with Hugh Bass. Preferably without Pam in the room.

By the time Dr. Bass returned to the room, Pam was done. She seemed to have every intention of standing there in the room, too. Dr. Bass greeted her again, got Myrtle to open her mouth and close it again while he checked her teeth and the x-rays that Pam had taken earlier. "Everything looks fine, Mrs. Clover, just fine."

Myrtle beamed at him and then looked at Pam. "Could you get me a cup of water, missy? My throat's gone completely dry." Two could play at the name-calling game.

Pam apparently didn't take kindly to being called missy. "There's a water fountain on the way out the door," she said a bit sourly.

Dr. Bass gave her a surprised look. "Pam, if you won't mind? Mrs. Clover might prefer a cup. I'd get it myself, but I've got a bunch of patients waiting on me."

Pam stoically trudged out on the errand.

Myrtle quickly said, "That's good of her. I've had such a week! I guess you must have heard about the tragic events at my house." Dr. Bass blinked at her. "The body in my backyard?"

"Was that in your yard? I heard the story, but didn't realize it had happened to you. Oh, that must have been a shock. I can only imagine." Dr. Bass wasn't looking directly at her.

Myrtle put what she hoped looked like a frail hand to her heart. "It was a terrible shock, yes. Dr. Bass, I do believe you knew the gentleman who was dead in my yard."

Now Hugh Bass was the one who looked shocked. "No. No, I don't think I did."

"Didn't Charles Clayborne grow up here in Bradley? And aren't you about the same age?"

Dr. Bass quickly doubled back. "Oh, him. Yes, I remember now. He went to school with me. But I haven't seen or talked to him for almost twenty years."

"Really?" Myrtle tilted her head to one side and appraised the dentist until he shifted uncomfortably. "By the way, did you know that I'm investigating the murder? For the paper, you know. I'm one of the reporters on staff."

Dr. Bass said quickly, "Well now. That's very interesting, Mrs. Clover. How nice for you to stay busy like that. Active minds and bodies are healthy minds and bodies." He gave her a rather condescending smile.

Pam sullenly entered the room again with the cup of water and Dr. Bass looked vastly relieved. He said in a suddenly perky voice, now that his escape was assured, "I'd better see to those other patients now. Mrs. Clover, I hope your week ends up going much more smoothly. Your teeth are in wonderful shape, so that news should help get you on the right track again." He gave her a quick wave and disappeared out the door, leaving Myrtle with Pam and a whole cup of water to drink.

Why did Dr. Bass lie about talking to Charles?

The next morning, Myrtle was on the phone early. Lee Woosley was supposed to come by to do his repairs and she needed to get hold of Puddin to get the rest of her cleaning done. If she were going to host people after the funeral, she didn't need to have dust bunnies chasing each other around the house.

As the phone rang and rang on Puddin's end, Myrtle thought again how quickly she'd fire Puddin if given the shot at a decent housekeeper. But really, since Puddin and Dusty were a package deal, she couldn't fire Puddin unless she had a guaranteed arrangement with a housekeeper *and* a yardman. Considering that both vocations were scarcer than hen's teeth in Bradley, she had a feeling that she wouldn't live to see the day.

As usual, Dusty picked up. When he heard her voice, he bayed his customary, "Too hot to mow, Miz Myrtle!"

"It's not either. I don't know why you always try putting off doing my yard, Dusty. You actually do a good job when you put your mind to it."

There was grumbling on the other end. "Just put me through to Puddin, then," said Myrtle with a sigh. Some days it was difficult to even try to communicate with Dusty. Finally, Puddin picked up. Myrtle said, "Puddin, I need you and Dusty back over here today to finish up the job you started. My yard is half done and my house isn't even a fraction of the way done and I've got company coming over soon. What time this morning will you come by?"

She steeled herself for the ridiculous answer that she knew was coming.

"Can't come," said Puddin with surly satisfaction. "We're on vacation, Dusty and me."

"Vacation? You and Dusty?" This boggled Myrtle's mind. "Aren't you picking up on your house phone right now?" Vacation? Puddin always flatly stated that they didn't have any money at all.

"We won a trip from the grocery store. We was their millionth customer," said Puddin smugly as if she'd planned it the whole time. "So we're about to walk out the door for our free trip."

This was just as ridiculous as Puddin's statement that they were on vacation. The grocery store in downtown Bradley had been open as long as Myrtle could remember. It *was* a small town, so perhaps it did take eighty years or so for it to reach a million customers. It seemed highly unlikely, however, that they would be taking count that long.

"Here in Bradley?" asked Myrtle.

"No, in Simonton. They have the big store."

Indeed they did. That would explain it.

"We're going to Myrtle Beach," said Puddin proudly. "Leaving today and won't come back for four days. So I can't clean your place. Good luck with the evil at your house and the bodies and stuff."

"There was only one body and you know it, Puddin," growled Myrtle. "Don't think you're getting off the hook. When you come back from the beach, I'm expecting you and Dusty over here immediately to finish the job. Besides, Dusty left his shovel over here."

"We'll get it later. Just stick it in your garage somewheres." Apparently, that was the end of the conversation because Puddin abruptly hung up.

Thirty minutes later, Myrtle glanced around her living room and kitchen. It didn't sparkle, but it wasn't dusty, either. She'd dug out a long-handled duster and found the attachments for the vacuum cleaner. She'd done probably as good a job as Puddin would have done and with the minimum of stooping. Now the yard was a different matter. That grass was pretty tall and it was just going to have to stay tall until Dusty got back.

Now that she'd expended so much effort into cleaning, a third attempt at watching her taped soap opera was in order. Maybe she could just fast-forward through the completely unbelievable hospital scenes when those came up. She fast-forwarded the show until she saw Jim and Bob having a serious discussion about Trina's involvement in the cult. She sighed in anticipation, snuggled down into the armchair, and promptly fell asleep.

The doorbell jolted her awake and she looked around her for her cane. She'd also apparently gotten molded into the armchair during her nap, and she was having a hard time getting out of the chair. There was a tap at the door and she hollered that she was coming, which wasn't really the truth, since she couldn't get the momentum to propel herself up.

Lee Woosley cautiously opened the front door and stuck his head in. Had she forgotten to lock the door? Good thing that it wasn't Red there or he'd have had her head. "Mrs. Clover?" His cautious look relaxed when he saw her in the chair. "Having a nap, were you?" He glanced at the television, "In front of your soap? See, that's what I'm looking forward to for retirement. Taking naps in front of junky shows on TV."

He came in and Myrtle felt a bit depressed that she'd taught someone who was getting close to retirement age. Lee must be about sixty or sixty-one now. He was a spindly man, but a wiry one. His hair was salt-and-pepper colored, heavy on the salt.

Lee's assumption that Myrtle's day revolved around naps and television annoyed her, but she was still waking up and decided to let it pass. She needed this man to open up to her and if she started out acting defensive, it probably wasn't going to help matters much. Myrtle gave a grimacing smile, "That's right. Thanks for coming by, Lee. Here, I made a small list of the things that I needed fixing." Of course, the list was on a table out of arm's reach. She was still looking in irritation for the cane. How could the stupid thing disappear like that? Half the time, it acted like it was trying to spite her.

Lee walked over and reached under her armchair and pulled out her cane, handing it to her. "Here you are, Mrs. Clover. Looks like it somehow slid all the way under your chair."

"Thanks," she said, finally pushing herself out of the chair's too-clingy embrace. She grabbed the list and handed it to Lee, then said, "I'll show you around the house. It's all fairly self-explanatory, though."

"Okay," said Lee. He hesitated, then said, "You know, it looks like you need help with the yard and all, too. Your grass looks like it hasn't been cut for a while. I know Red is busy—do you have someone to do yard work for you?"

Myrtle tottered for a second in surprise, then clasped her hands together over the top of the cane. "Lee! You're...you're not a yardman, are you? Do you do yards?" The thought of gleefully firing the resentful Dusty and impossible Puddin made her want to chortle with delight.

"No, I'm afraid I don't," said Lee quickly. "But I just noticed that it looked like you needed help. I could call around and see if there's anybody looking to make some money on the side."

"Thanks," said Myrtle. She'd already written off that offer. There'd been a time when she'd had to piece together yard service among different men who needed a few extra dollars. It was even harder to get a regular schedule of mowing that way than it was to put up with Dusty. At least Dusty came regularly. The problem was that no one besides Dusty was willing to weed-eat around her gnome collection. It was a pity.

"Since I haven't seen you in so many years, Lee," said Myrtle, "why don't you catch me up to speed. You've got a family?"

Lee hesitated. "Actually, my wife died some time back. But I do have my daughter, Peggy. And a granddaughter, too. My granddaughter is almost eighteen now."

"Oh, that's nice. Of course—I know Peggy. And her husband...let's see. What's his name again?"

Lee said, "She was married to Jim Neighbors, but they divorced a long time ago." He shifted uncomfortably, as if the topic pained him. "But it looks like she might start dating the dentist here—Hugh Bass."

"Really? That's nice," repeated Myrtle.

Lee was eager to move to other topics. Myrtle got the strong sensation that he was a very old-fashioned man with old-fashioned views on marriage and divorce. "And how is *your* family going, Mrs. Clover? Red's doing all right, I guess?"

This seemed like it might make a good time to segue into talking about the case. "Well, Red's all right. He's real busy right now, though. You know."

Lee didn't seem to know much, actually. He cocked his head to one side and looked at her with a blank expression. "Is he? Why is that? Those kids pulling fire alarm levers at the city hall again?"

Myrtle stared at him. He couldn't be the only man in the town of Bradley not to know about the murder. So why was he playing dumb?

"No, Lee. I mean with the murder. There was a man murdered a couple of days ago. In my backyard, as a matter of fact."

"Oh. *Him*." Lee gave a shrug of a bony shoulder, but there was a ruddy flush working up his face and Myrtle knew he was feeling stronger emotions than he was letting on. "I guess that would be bringing him some extra work, wouldn't it?"

Myrtle said, "It was the most remarkable thing, Lee. Here I was, minding my own business, and the yardman discovers a body nestled right out there with my gnomes. It was quite disturbing. Especially since I'd never laid eyes on this man before. Had you? Red seemed to think you'd had some sort of argument with him recently."

Now there was more reaction from him. His eyes narrowed. "I reckon that I did, Mrs. Clover. I didn't know the fellow very well myself, but he tried to cheat me at a poker game the other night. My buddies and I play cards fair, and that's all there is to it. He acted like some kind of card shark and stole money from us just as surely as if he'd picked our pockets. I beat the stuffing out of him and he deserved every bit of it, and more."

"Did you know anything else about this man? Other than the fact that he cheated at cards?" asked Myrtle.

"I know that he was a bad guy, through and through. I'm not crying any tears over his death and I don't think anybody who knew him is. For a guy who wasn't in town very long, he sure did create trouble," he said.

"What else made him a bad guy?" persisted Myrtle.

Lee hesitated. "Just a feeling I have."

"Apparently he grew up here," pressed Myrtle. "Did you know him then at all?"

Lee's lips were sealed, though. All he'd say was, "We'd better get on with your list, Mrs. Clover. I've got a couple of people to see after you. Besides, what's in the past is in the past."

But Myrtle knew, from her vast experience in life, that the past was rarely ever truly in the past.

Chapter Seven

Since Myrtle wasn't completely satisfied with the result of her talk with Lee, she conveniently forgot to mention a few of the projects on her list. She was going to need an excuse to get the man back over to her house. He ended up surprising her by having done a very careful, thorough job with the repairs that she did give him to finish. The only thing that he hadn't fixed was the planter that needed to be reattached to the back wall of the house—he hadn't had the right screws. Red would be pleased, thought Myrtle as she watched Lee wave to her while carefully making his way through the maze of gnomes to his aging pickup truck.

Red *was* pleased. He ended up knocking on her door just an hour after Lee left. She showed him the work he'd done and Red nodded his head. "He didn't charge you much, either," he said, glancing at the invoice on Myrtle's desk. "I might have to have him come over to my house and do some stuff for me, too. He could probably knock out half of my list in no time."

Myrtle nodded, only half listening. "Do you have a few minutes, Red? To help me out?"

Red looked loath to commit since he wasn't sure what she was going to ask him to do. "Actually, Mama, I came by to ask you a couple of questions regarding the murder."

Myrtle perked up. Questions meant that she could draw inferences. He must really have some new evidence for him to show his hand that way. But she still needed to have a ride to and from the grocery store. There were lots of things she needed to buy for that reception and she wasn't going to be able to carry more than one bag and her cane at the same time.

"You can ask me all about it on the way to the grocery store and back," said Myrtle.

Red relaxed. "Oh, you just need to go to the store? No problem. I thought you were going to ask me to mow that grass of yours and I've got too much to do with this case." Myrtle reached for her cane and her pocketbook while Red looked out her window at the grass, which threatened to obliterate the gnomes from view. "What on earth happened to Dusty? He's not usually so slack."

"He won some kind of trip to the beach and he and Puddin have taken off for a few days," grumbled Myrtle as they headed out her front door, locking it carefully behind them. "It's too bad, but there's no way around it." She paused and then said, "What did you need to ask me about?"

"The day of the murder, did you notice a woman hanging around our street?" asked Red. They walked across the street to his driveway and he held open the front door of the police car for her.

Myrtle frowned. "Well, sure I did. Erma, for one. She's always lurking around hoping to ambush me and tell me all about her latest fungal infection or something equally revolting. Elaine was hanging out in your front yard, pushing Jack in the toddler swing. Old Franny Parsons staggered to her mailbox and back about a million times. I guess she was trying to see if her pension check had arrived. And...."

Red started up the car and backed it out into the street. "I mean, did you see a woman hanging around our street that you wouldn't ordinarily expect to see."

"Like...of what description, Red? I can't immediately think of someone, no." It irritated her to think that she'd let some sort of major clue slip by her.

"Well, from what I hear, she'd have been very thin. Rough looking. Wild black hair," recited Red.

"Nicotine-stained hands and missing teeth?" asked Myrtle quickly.

Red nodded, glancing intently her way as he headed toward downtown. "That's the one. So you saw her? What time did you see her?"

"No, I didn't see her," said Myrtle quite truthfully. She just happened to know whom he was referring to, that was all.

"Then how could you describe her if you didn't see her?" asked Red through gritted teeth.

"Just a guess, that's all. I used my imagination and hit the nail on the head," said Myrtle, not as truthfully this time. She knew this was a description of Wanda, the psychic who lived in a shack on the way out of town. What on earth Wanda would have been doing on their street, she had no idea, but it was too coincidental not to have something to do with the murder. As soon as she could catch a ride from Miles, she'd be out there getting the full story from her.

Red looked suspicious. "I don't recall your being particularly fanciful before, Mama. Are you sure you don't know anything about this woman?"

"Not a bit." Mercifully, they were parking outside the store now and Red was helping her out the door. She got a cart and they went inside.

Myrtle walked over to the dairy counter and piled cheese into her cart. Red blinked at her. "Mama, why are you buying all this cheese? You won't be able to eat it all before it goes bad."

"I'm hosting a reception after Charles Clayborne's funeral," said Myrtle. "Remember? To be a good friend to Miles, you know. Since it's his cousin's funeral and the service is here in Bradley and since Miles doesn't want to host anything or really even claim the man as kin." She moved her cart to a center aisle and pulled out a few boxes of gelatin in different colors.

Myrtle glanced at Red. "Why are you making a face like that?"

"This is the food you're serving at the funeral reception? Cheese and gelatin?" he asked.

"Well, not together! But, yes. I'm going to cut the cheese into cubes and put it on a big plate. And the gelatin I'll put in a big bowl and people can help themselves," said Myrtle.

Red cleared his throat and stared into the grocery cart at the offending items. "Mama, have you gone to any funeral receptions lately? I don't think I've seen much cheese and gelatin at the ones I've been to."

"Cut to the chase, Red. What are you saying? That I don't need to buy this stuff?"

"Or maybe that you should get some different things. Won't the church be sending food over to Miles? Usually the church ladies always show up with ham biscuits, deviled eggs, potato salad, peach cobbler—stuff like that," said Red.

"I can make deviled eggs," said Myrtle, feeling stubborn. Why was everyone always in such a tizzy when she mentioned she was having a reception? She strongly suspected it was age-discrimination, a frequent suspicion of hers considering her relentless inching toward ninety. Ninety-year-olds didn't get the proper respect. Octogenarians still commanded their share of power.

"Sure you can," said Red, rolling his eyes. "But why even bother when you'll be receiving food from the church, anyway? You're helping out enough just hosting everyone in your house."

It could be that she wanted to bother simply because everyone seemed so dead-set against her doing it. "I'm already at the store, Red. I've heard your advice and I won't make quite as much food as I planned to make, but I can't just hold a reception and wait for the food to show up. I've also got to make sure there's something to drink there."

"Well, do me a favor and keep it alcohol-free. After breaking up that drunken brawl up last week, all I want is to make sure the town of Bradley is drinking lemonade," said Red.

"I was only planning on serving non-alcoholic drinks," said Myrtle primly. "But I think you've lost your mind if you think that people are going to fight at a funeral reception."

The next morning, Myrtle picked up the phone and dialed Miles. His very sleepy voice answered after six or seven rings.

"Are you sleeping?" asked Myrtle with great surprise.

"Not any longer," said Miles in a cold voice.

"I figured you'd have been up for hours," said Myrtle, feeling a slight pang of remorse. Still, crime fighting didn't stop for the clock and she had investigating to do early.

Miles gave only a grumpy-sounding snort in response.

"The reason I'm calling is that I need to drive out to see Wanda this morning. Red said she'd been lurking around our street before the murder and I want to find out what she was doing. So, I need to either borrow your car or hitch a ride with you out to her place," said Myrtle.

Miles heaved a long-suffering type of sigh. "This is the psychic out on the old highway, heading out of town? The one who lives with her insane brother?"

"Crazy like a fox, if you ask me. Yes, he's called Crazy Dan," said Myrtle.

"Can't you ask someone else for a ride," asked Miles in annoyance. "You've gotten rides from others before. Like Erma."

Myrtle said with dignity, "I'll pretend you didn't say that. As you well know, I've been avoiding Erma like the plague for some time. Deliberately seeking out her company would mean that I'd had a small stroke. Besides, the last time I saw her—from a distance—she was babbling incoherently about having a clue...that you were the murderer."

Miles groaned. "Typical. And I suppose she'll blab whatever nonsense she's got fixed in her head to everyone in town. There goes my reputation. Miles Bradford—murderer."

"Not necessarily. No one listens to Erma Sherman anyway. For their own self-protection. Otherwise, their heads would explode with all her disgusting medical reports on her various revolting conditions. Besides, knowing the old hens in this town, the thought of you being some sort of rogue would make you even more appealing," said Myrtle.

"You mean adding to my appeal as someone who still drives," said Miles dryly. For some reason, the thought he was desirable simply because of his driver's license had certainly stung.

"Going back to my need for a ride. Erma is impossible to ask because she's so infernally nosy," said Myrtle.

Miles gave a suggestive cough.

"I know what you're thinking. But I'm investigating, not being nosy. I've already written a short update story for the paper. It's running tomorrow morning." It wasn't a really newsy article since there weren't a lot of undisputed facts about the case yet. But the important thing was that the story had her byline on it. She could use the investigative reporter angle to question suspects anytime she needed to.

"Whatever," sighed Miles. "I guess I could drive you out there in a little while. It'll at least give me an excuse not to endure a visit from Aunt Connie. She said she might drop by this afternoon."

"Really?" asked Myrtle. "Oh, Miles, we shouldn't pass up a chance to talk with her. If we go to Wanda's house this morning, that leaves all afternoon for us to talk to Aunt Connie."

"You won't enjoy the experience Myrtle. You'll want to run away. It'll be very similar to a visit with Erma Sherman."

"I doubt that very much," said Myrtle firmly. "Besides, I usually hit it off with the elderly. I'm a member of the club, after all."

"Yes, you've been a card-carrying member for a few years," said Miles. "But remember—she's not particularly elderly. In fact, she's not even sixty."

"There's something really icky about that, too," said Myrtle distastefully. "Yuck."

"Nothing to do with me," said Miles. "My uncle just fancied much younger women. And I told you that I don't want to claim either my aunt or Cousin Charles. Now look, if we're going out into the sticks to visit a country psychic, I need to go ahead and get ready."

Myrtle snorted. "Don't worry about dressing up. We'll be lucky if Wanda is wearing shoes. And *very* lucky if Crazy Dan is wearing a shirt."

Miles sucked in a shuddering breath. "Fine. I'm *so* excited about the direction my day is heading. Maybe I'll forgo my coffee this morning and have a Bloody Mary instead."

"As long as I'm driving, which I'm happy to do. My driver's license is good for another decade."

Miles made a funny noise on his end of the phone, which she couldn't quite decipher. "Never mind. I'll just be sure to serve drinks while dear Aunt Connie is visiting. I'll need one then."

An hour later, Miles pulled his car up in front of Myrtle's house. She grabbed her cane, locked the door behind her, and started carefully picking her way through the now very tall grass and gnomes. One of the problems was that her yard was afflicted with crabgrass. She glared resentfully at Erma Sherman's offending yard, the source of the scourge. If Myrtle just had regular grass in her yard, it would never be this tall now. That Erma! And that Puddin and Dusty, too!

She jumped when a nasal voice whispered out her name and held her cane up, protectively. Sure enough, it was Erma. "You scared the living daylights out of me," she snapped at her neighbor. "What are you whispering about? All I need is to fall down in this death trap of a yard, thinking I'm hearing ghosts."

Erma's eyes were large and she bobbed her head in the direction of Miles's car. "You're not going off with *him* are you? Myrtle, you're in danger."

"He's not that bad of a driver. I'm only in fair-to-middling danger. I'm in a lot more danger than that just walking around my yard right now. Can you do something about the crabgrass situation? It's spilling over into my yard and turning it into a disaster area," said Myrtle.

Erma looked around Myrtle's yard and smirked. "Ha! Your yard is a disaster area, crabgrass or no crabgrass. You're going off on a tangent, too. I wasn't talking about Miles's driving; I was talking about the fact that he's a deranged killer." Her donkey-like face focused intently on Myrtle.

Myrtle waved her cane in the air, hoping at least to make Erma back up a bit so her fetid breath wouldn't waft in her direction. "All right. You've warned me. Now let me catch up with my ride."

Erma looked tenderly at her. "I know you have feelings for Miles, but you can't let your romantic dreams get in the way of your safety. Are you usually drawn to dangerous men?"

Myrtle roared at her and stomped away. "Enough of your nonsense! I am *not* in love with Miles Bradford!"

She yanked open the passenger side door, plopped herself inside, and slammed the door behind her.

"I never imagined that you were," said Miles mildly.

Myrtle noticed the car windows were down. She huffily rolled hers back up. "Erma has gone too far this time. Too far!"

Miles sighed. "What kind of rumors will she be responsible for circulating this time?"

"Aside from the one she's already propagating—your being a vicious killer? I'm sure she's reviving her favorite rumor...that you and I are involved," said Myrtle grumpily.

"No one pays attention to that one anyway," said Miles.

"Hmph," said Myrtle.

They rode in silence for a couple of minutes, then Miles said, "Can you remind me again where this place is? I know it's on the old highway out of town, but that's all I remember."

"It's a ways out. Just keep driving. You'll start to see signs advising you to examine the state of your soul, then you'll see signs for *boil p-nuts, bait, and sykick.* That's when you'll need to slow down to turn off," said Myrtle.

"I can hardly wait," said Miles grimly.

It was a good twenty-five minutes before they started seeing the signs off the badly potholed state highway outside Bradley. "These aren't so bad," said Miles. "Jesus loves you? That's a lovely sentiment, Myrtle."

"Just wait."

The next sign was a bit more ominous. *Forbidden fruit creates many jams.* "Well, it's certainly true. The straight and narrow path usually leads to an uncomplicated life. I think these rural churches are simply looking out for their parishioners."

Myrtle grunted.

The next sign said: *Choose the bread of life or you are toast,* followed quickly by: *Eternity is a long time to be wrong.*

Miles heaved another sigh. He seemed to be full of them lately.

"Right here," said Myrtle pointing off to the side of the road where a faded sign advertised bait, hubcaps, peanuts, and psychic readings for sale.

"Where's the house?" asked Miles, pulling into the dirt and gravel path (that was heavy on dirt and low on gravel) that passed for a driveway and carefully dodging various cars on cinderblocks.

"Right there in front of you! Don't tell me you can't see it," said Myrtle, waving a hand at a shack that was completely engulfed in hubcaps.

Miles blinked at the shack. "I assumed that was the hubcap showroom. They live there?"

"Oh, it's fine. Don't be such a priss. I'm sure there are probably many advantages in living in a house covered by hubcaps."

"So," said Miles slowly, "when a customer *wants* a new hubcap, they pull it off their house?" He seemed unduly concerned about the structure of the house. It must be his engineering background. Or whatever it is that he used to do.

"Come on, let's go up there," said Myrtle, impatiently, pulling her cane out of the backseat and heaving herself out of the car. She walked over to the house and rapped her cane on one of the hubcaps. There was a sign duct-taped near the door that said, *Madam Zora. Sykick. Tarro Card reeding.*

"Crazy Dan always is the one who answers," grumbled Myrtle. "For some reason he acts personally offended whenever he sees me at the door."

A grizzled man with leathery skin and days of stubble yanked the door open abruptly and glanced suspiciously at both; then his beady eyes honed back in on Myrtle. "You! What're you doing here again?"

Chapter Eight

"For heaven's sake! I haven't been here for months, Crazy Dan. You act like I'm down here every week panhandling or something." Myrtle frowned at the scraggly man who indeed was not wearing a shirt. "Is Wanda in today?"

The man tilted his head to the side. "Whassat?"

"I said is Wanda in," said Myrtle loudly. Noting the look of confusion still on the man's face, she said again, "*Wand-er*. Your sister."

"Need a for-toon read?" Now Crazy Dan looked cunning.

Myrtle knew she hadn't brought any money with her. She turned to give Miles an inquiring stare.

Miles sighed. "I suppose so."

Crazy Dan nodded and took to gazing at Miles's carefully pressed golf shirt, khaki pants, and nice shoes. "Wander!" he hollered. With the shack as tiny as it was, it was hard to imagine that a raised voice was even necessary.

He disappeared into the dark depths of the shack and Wanda appeared. She looked exactly as Red had described and Myrtle gave a satisfied nod. Nicotine stains, bedraggled hair. Leathery, sun-ripened skin. Really just a female version of Crazy Dan. Fortunately, she *was* wearing a shirt and even wore a pair of disreputable-looking bedroom slippers. She didn't seem surprised to see them at all.

"Wondered when you'd come," she said in a dissolute voice, turning to walk into the shack. Myrtle supposed they were intended to follow her, so she carefully entered into the darkness. Going from the broad, unrelenting daylight to the dimness of the cluttered house might be a recipe for disaster. Myrtle poked in front of her with her cane to make sure she wasn't going to trip over piles of laundry or psychic accoutrements or perhaps spare hubcaps.

Fastidious Miles didn't look as if he particularly wanted to sit down on Madam Zora's sofa. He appeared concerned about the cleanliness of the conditions. "I've been driving for a while so I might just stand and stretch my legs for a bit."

Myrtle wondered if Wanda saw straight through that statement. Wanda studied Miles through narrowed eyes. She let it pass without a challenge and said, "Come to get your for-toon read?"

Myrtle said warily, "I told Dan I would, but I'm not too sure about that, Wanda. That never ends up going well."

"Why not?" asked Miles, eyes still glancing into the corners of the room as if watching for rodents to leap out at him.

"Because she always sees horrible things. Horrible. She's never looked at my palm and said, 'You'll win a million dollars in the sweepstakes and be happy for the rest of your life.' It's always something completely ghastly that she says."

"Not fair," said Wanda. "I just read what's there. Give me a chance and mebbe there won't be bad stuff now."

Myrtle sighed and held out her hand. Wanda took it, looked into her palm and muttered, "Death." She dropped Myrtle's hand as if it burned her, then lit up a cigarette.

"See!" demanded Myrtle furiously.

Miles said dubiously, "But that's not really even a stretch of your imagination is it, Wanda? Considering the customer, I mean." Myrtle shot him an angry look and he blushed. "I mean, well, considering her age...um...well...her advancing years...."

Myrtle gave him a repressive glare. "How *gallant* of you, Miles. Eighty is the new seventy, you know."

"But you're not eighty. You're nearly ninety," said Miles, confused, before blushing even more furiously than before.

Wanda said scornfully, "Didn't predict it because she's *old*. There's other death 'round her—not natural, either. And danger. I always warn her. Never listens."

Miles nodded sympathetically.

"Maybe," said Myrtle in an irritated voice, "the reason you're seeing death everywhere is because you recently murdered someone."

Miles gave a choking laugh at her directness.

"Whadya mean?" Wanda's eyes narrowed. "I ain't done nothin.'" She blew a blue cloud of cigarette smoke at Myrtle's face.

"Are you sure? Because you were seen lurking on my street near my house the night a murder was committed. In my backyard." Myrtle steadily held the psychic's gaze.

"Wasn't there at night!" interjected Wanda hotly, then glared resentfully at Myrtle for having tricked her into disclosing that she'd been there at all.

"Why were you there?" asked Myrtle. "What were you doing hanging out around my house?"

"Didn't even know it was *yer* house!" said Wanda.

"You're the psychic! You should know stuff like that," said Myrtle.

"That's a little detail. I don't get little details," said Wanda in a defensive voice. "And the reason I was in your area is because I had a vision." She stubbed out her cigarette and put her skinny hands on her emaciated hips.

"What sort of a vision?" asked Miles, curiously. He'd been busy the last few minutes looking around Wanda's living room at the crystal ball, Tarot cards, and other oddities. Maybe he missed his calling as a seer instead of being an architect. Or whatever it was that he used to do.

Wanda turned to stare at him. "Thought you was going to be hurt," she told Miles. "In the vision, you was going to be hurt. I thought I'd go over there and stop it. I should know better than to mess with the stars, though."

"You thought that *I* was going to be hurt?" asked Miles, startled. "Why on earth would you have a vision like that?"

"He was up to no good," said Wanda, giving a shiver. "No good, that Cousin Charles."

Now she had Miles's complete attention. "How do you know Cousin Charles?" asked Miles intently. His eyes were wide with what looked like terror as he waited for the answer.

"Because he's kin."

"Kin to *whom*?" Miles's eyes were saucers behind his wire-rimmed glasses.

"To me. To you." Wanda said it simply, giving Miles a world-weary look.

"But how?" Miles's white face indicated that he was in desperate need of that Bloody Mary he'd been talking about earlier.

Wanda shrugged a bony shoulder and seemed disinclined to answer.

Myrtle persisted with her line of questioning. "So you went over to Miles's house and hung out for a while to see what you could see? What *did* you see?"

Wanda said, "The vision was fuzzy on the time. Must have been the wrong time. Didn't see Cousin Charles."

"Did you see anything else?" asked Myrtle, ignoring the fact that Miles was muttering something under his breath.

Wanda stared at Myrtle. "Just yer cat." She looked away and Myrtle swore she was hiding something. So she'd seen something but didn't want to share it. Great. What was it about the people involved with this case? None of them wanted to talk.

Miles was once again in charge of the conversation, but Myrtle had already lost interest since it was clear that Wanda wasn't going to share any more information. At least not today.

"If you could just tell me," pleaded Miles, "*exactly* how we're related?"

In the car, as they headed back from Wanda and Crazy Dan's shack, the fact that Miles asked Myrtle to drive him home was a strong indication of just how shaken up he was. Myrtle set off at a stately thirty-five miles per hour. "What on earth were you thinking, Miles, asking Wanda to the funeral? And my reception!"

Miles was blindly staring out at the slowly passing landscape in a dazed fashion. "Well. She's family, after all. I've got to observe all the niceties."

"Family in a very convoluted way, and only because your uncle was a miscreant. What a reprobate to saddle Crazy Dan and Wanda's mother with two children and then not provide care for them!" replied Myrtle, veering off the road just a hair while overcome by emotion.

Miles buried his head in his hands. "Oh Myrtle. That's right—Crazy Dan is related to me, too."

"Let's not fall apart over it all, Miles. It's not as if you have to suddenly start going over to visit them on Sunday afternoons after church or anything. Just carry on as usual. You're not even claiming the other members of your family in the area, anyway. What's two more cousins?" asked Myrtle. Then she turned grim. "But you didn't invite Crazy Dan to my reception, I hope. He never wears a shirt!"

Miles spoke out of the depths of his hands again. "I didn't specifically tell Wanda to come with her brother, no. Who knows if he'll decide to show up? I don't even know how Wanda got over to our street on the night of the murder. All the cars I saw were up on cinder blocks."

"I guess there must be one that actually works." Again she glanced over at Miles, who really did appear to be having some sort of terrible headache or attack of some kind. "Don't be so worried, Miles! Everything is going to be fine."

The *everything is fine* mantra was one that Myrtle continued repeating when she'd finally gotten back home. Here she was with a reception going on the next day and she felt extremely unprepared. For one thing, she'd forgotten to get flowers at the store for that simple memorial she was trying to create, and the flowers in her yard weren't looking so great right now.

Myrtle peered out her side window into Erma's backyard to see if her roses were still as ratty as ever. As expected, the poor things looked as if they were positively gasping for water.

She snapped her fingers. But in his yard, Miles had that huge magnolia tree that completely overshadowed his backyard. Myrtle would be over there this afternoon when Miles's aunt came over to visit. She could pull off a blossom or two and float them in a big bowl outside.

She then turned her attention to her house. It looked all right, she guessed. She knew the hall bathroom could use a cleaning before tomorrow and her kitchen would need cleaning after she finished cooking.

Something else was bothering her. Whenever she talked about the funeral reception, people kept mentioning ham biscuits. She hadn't picked up any ham when she was at the store with Red and the only biscuits she could competently handle were the kind that came out of a can. Apparently, this ham-at-funeral-receptions-thing was practically as sacred a tradition as having ham at Easter.

There was no way around it—she'd have to go back to the store. Sighing deeply, she grabbed a bag and her cane and headed out the door. At least she'd figured out the flower situation. There was no way she'd be able to carry a ham, flowers, and a cane.

Roy, the butcher, winced as he saw Myrtle Clover coming up. He was well-acquainted with the lady from years of her frequenting his meat counter. He was of the opinion that she was an excellent English teacher, but a terrible cook. Roy always felt guilty, sending off a poor, unsuspecting cut of meat home with her.

Today it was ham that was on her mind. He didn't think he'd ever sold her a ham before. He felt a strange reluctance to do so now.

She was frowning at him, hunching over on her cane as if it had been a long day already. She was a formidable old woman with a towering six-foot height and a towering intellect, too. And she was already unhappy with him. He suddenly realized she'd been talking to him and he'd been too deep in his thoughts to hear her.

"I need a ham," she repeated, now getting that stern look he remembered from the times he'd forgotten to bring in his English homework.

"Of course, Mrs. Clover," he said meekly. "How much do you need?"

"I'm thinking fifteen pounds," she said.

Roy got the ham out, came around the side of the counter, and placed the ham tenderly in her cart for her. "Now," he said slowly, "do you need any...well, helpful hints for the ham?"

She gave him more of the steely glare. "I think I can handle the ham, Roy. I'll cook it and be just fine."

He continued feeling this strong sense of responsibility toward the meat. She did know it was fully cooked, right? "It really just needs warming or maybe a glaze...." At the look she was giving him, he broke off. Well, it wasn't going to be his fault, was it? He looked sadly after her as she walked away, leaning heavily on her cart.

Really! Roy seemed in league with everyone else in town who thought she couldn't host a simple funeral reception. This made her even more determined to have everything go smoothly and catch the murderer simultaneously. She thumped down the sidewalk toward her house, thinking about the case as she went. It must be time for Miles's aunt to come by for the visit by now. Maybe she should stick the ham in the oven before she went over there. She would be very close by, after all.

At home, she put the ham on the table and looked at the label. Slightly over fifteen pounds. From what she remembered from the last time she'd hosted Thanksgiving (another occasion when no one appeared to accept that she knew what she was doing), she'd had a bird a pound or so bigger than this ham. It had taken much longer for the turkey to cook than she'd planned on and she'd had to come up with reasons for the delay that didn't involve the fact that the turkey wasn't cooked. Myrtle wasn't about to make the same mistake of underestimating the cooking time again. At least it wasn't frozen...that was a bonus, especially considering the fact that the reception was tomorrow afternoon.

Myrtle thoughtfully considered the oven. Had it been 375 degrees that she'd cooked that turkey on? She thought so. She preheated the oven and unwrapped the ham and placed it in a pan. It seemed to come with a glaze. How convenient! Would that taste good in the biscuits, though? It should, shouldn't it? She mixed up the glaze according to the directions and never saw the directions that came for warming the ham.

Once the oven preheated, she put the ham in and picked up the phone to call Miles.

"Is she there yet?" asked Myrtle, still breathless from the exertion of going to the store and manhandling the ham.

"Not yet," said Miles with a sigh. "I'm really not up to seeing her now."

"Are you planning on mentioning Wanda and Crazy Dan to her?"

"Why would she even care? It was something her father-in-law did ages ago," said Miles.

"Okay. I'm heading over," said Myrtle, hanging up. She picked up her cane and glanced at herself in the mirror. Her white hair was standing up like Einstein, so she impatiently patted it down before walking out the door.

She and Miles were on their second glass of wine and still no aunt.

"She did say she was coming, didn't she?" asked Myrtle. "Our waiting is causing me to drink more wine than I'd planned on doing."

Miles shrugged. "It's not like we're driving anywhere. It's been a long day for me."

"It's been a long day for me, and I still have a bunch of stuff to do," said Myrtle. "Cleaning and cooking. And I need to take a couple of magnolia blossoms off your tree for my memorial in the backyard."

Miles gave a choking chortle that was most unlike him. Myrtle raised her eyebrows and wondered if Miles had started with the wine before she arrived. "The memorial, right," he said. "Can you reach the blossoms on the tree? I was just thinking about you climbing trees at your age."

Myrtle shot him a cold stare. "I'm very tall, as you know, so I'm sure I won't have any problems. For heaven's sake, Miles."

It was probably fortunate that the doorbell rang at that moment. She was starting to get really irritated with Miles but she didn't have the luxury of stomping off in a huff.

Miles's Aunt Connie looked to be in her late fifties and bore absolutely no resemblance to him whatsoever. She had a dissatisfied mouth, a weak chin, and small eyes that right now glanced around Miles's house suspiciously, as if speculating that he housed many family mementoes that should be in her home, instead.

"Oh Miles, isn't it terrible? Our poor, poor Charles! I just haven't even absorbed the news at all. To have his life ended so young and when he was so full of promise!"

Miles frowned doubtfully at both the youth and the promise of his cousin, but he was too polite to do anything but give a hesitant nod. "Is everything coming together for the funeral?" he asked stiffly, motioning to his aunt to take a seat.

Connie plopped down on Miles's leather sofa, putting a hand out subconsciously to run along the expensive surface. "It's all right. There really wasn't much to do—just coordinate with the funeral home and plan the graveside service. They're taking it from there."

Miles said, "You know that Myrtle is hosting the reception after the funeral."

Connie's forehead furrowed in confusion.

"Myrtle. Right there," said Miles, gesturing at Myrtle.

Myrtle tried to smile graciously, despite just having been grievously ignored.

"Is she?" asked Connie doubtfully, tilting her head to one side. "Where does she live?"

Myrtle was unused to being talked about as if she wasn't in the same room. Her forced smile became more of a grimace as she gritted through her teeth. "I live only a few yards away. As a matter of fact, it was in my yard that your son met his untimely demise."

A spark of interest finally shone in Connie's eyes. "Did you happen to see anything? That night, I mean? Or hear anything?"

Myrtle cursed herself for the twentieth time for having such an unusual lapse of acuity the night of the murder. "I'm afraid I didn't. And I'm sorry for your loss."

Connie sniffed, thinking again of her recent tragedy. "Thank you. It's kind of you to host the reception." She paused. "I'm not sure how many people will be there. That makes it hard to plan."

Miles said, "I'm sure the ladies from my church will be bringing by some extra food the day of the funeral. We'll be fine."

Myrtle shifted restlessly. She was ready to get in the driver's seat with some questions herself. Connie had had control of this conversation long enough. "Miles was quite surprised that Charles was in town, Connie. Did you know that he was in Bradley?"

Connie blinked at her and quickly said, "Naturally. He came to visit me and then wanted to catch up with old high school friends who still lived in Bradley."

Myrtle got the distinct impression that she actually hadn't had the vaguest clue that he was in town. "Where had he been living before coming back to Bradley?" she asked.

"Oh, here and there," said Connie with a vague wave of her hand to demonstrate that Charles had sort of floated around in the ether.

"He was a drifter, then?" asked Myrtle innocently.

"Certainly not!" said Connie with a gasp at the word. "He was an adventurer. Charles loved experiencing *life*. That's why his death is such a tragedy."

"He was a world traveler?" asked Miles, sounding quite surprised. "I've done some traveling in my time—work-related, most of it. Where did he go?" Miles leaned forward on the sofa, looking at his aunt intently. His voice wasn't at all snarky. He couldn't possibly believe this tall tale of Connie's could he? Or, was Miles perhaps just a little bit tipsy?

"Charles was a very independent young man," said Connie stiffly. "He didn't find it necessary to discuss all his travels with his mother."

Which meant these travels were likely confined to North Carolina.

"What industry was Charles in?" asked Myrtle in her very sweetest tones. "Did business bring him to Bradley, or was his visit strictly to catch up with you and his friends?"

Connie pressed her thin lips together. Miles took another good-sized sip of wine and continued to forget to offer his aunt any. This was quite a stunning lapse for Miles and another sign of how shaken he was from the events of the day.

"He was an entrepreneur," said Connie. "He worked with start-up businesses. Very cutting-edge things that you and I wouldn't really understand."

In other words, he was chronically unemployed and constantly asking acquaintances to invest money in various shady operations.

"So he might have been in town to drum up support for a new business opportunity?" asked Myrtle.

Connie didn't make a snappy reply this time. There was, in fact, a distinct hesitation before she said, "No, remember? I said he was in town to catch up with me and with friends."

Miles said, "Do you have any idea why he'd be coming to see me so late at night, Connie?"

She raised her penciled-in eyebrows. "Was he coming to see you, Miles? I didn't know that." She looked at him suspiciously now.

"Well, he never *told* me he was coming to visit me. In fact, I had no idea that he was even in town. It does seem very late to be paying a visit," said Miles, backtracking now.

"Maybe he was coming to see me," said Myrtle with a shrug. "After all, he was in my yard, Miles, not yours."

"Why on earth would he have been coming to see you?" asked Connie with a short laugh. "No, he was probably meeting Miles. He might have realized he was finally being remiss about seeing his cousin."

Myrtle and Miles didn't point out that it was very odd timing finally to reach that conclusion.

"Did he tell you there was anyone in particular in Bradley that he was trying to catch up with?" asked Myrtle.

"No, I hadn't talked to Charles in a couple of weeks," said Connie.

"I thought you said that Charles had visited with you before his murder," said Myrtle, frowning.

Connie flushed an unattractive shade of crimson. "He was planning on coming by, of course. But circumstances obviously made that impossible." She sniffed again and looked as if the waterworks were in imminent threat of turning on again. "My poor Charles! Misunderstood and taken to heaven in the prime of his life!" She studied the ceiling as if looking for answers. "I wonder if I'll ever know what truly happened to him. Maybe I should offer a reward for information relating to his murder. It's simply so awful not knowing what *happened*." She rummaged in her patent-leather pocketbook and found a tissue, blowing her nose with gusto.

It was at this point that Myrtle decided that she should probably check on her ham. There was no way there was going to be any more information gotten from Miles's Aunt Connie. When she made her way out the door, an apprehensive-looking Miles was listening to his aunt wax poetic on what a dear boy Charles had always been. And she was pawing through her large pocketbook for photographs.

Myrtle was so eager to escape from Miles's house and his aunt's unfortunate predilection for son worshipping that she completely forgot about her nemesis. Naturally, Erma Sherman hadn't forgotten about *her*. When Myrtle had glimpsed her, it was already too late.

"Myrtle!" said Erma in a pleased voice. "I saw you go in Miles's house but I figured you probably wouldn't come back out for a while. I know how it is when you two visit each other. Although I still say you're taking your life in your hands just being around Miles."

"Sorry, Erma, I've got to run back to my house. I've got to get everything ready for the funeral reception tomorrow," said Myrtle.

She bit her wayward tongue fiercely when Erma said, "You're hosting the reception? Perfect! Of course I'll be there—I've got to support my neighbor. How is Miles holding up? Considering he's responsible."

"He's not at all responsible and he and Charles weren't close, so he isn't particularly devastated." She fished in her pocketbook for her keys, which apparently were determined to elude her desperate clutches.

Erma sniffed at the air with her well-developed nose. "Is that something burning that I smell? Yes! Yes, something's burning. You didn't leave something on the stove, did you?" She gaped at Myrtle's house and stepped back a notch as if concerned that the entire building was going to blow up.

Chapter Nine

Myrtle finally found her keys, thrust one into the lock, and pushed at the door. The inside of her house was foggy with smoke. She muttered imprecations and hurried to the kitchen.

Erma had a tissue over her nose and screeched, "Myrtle! Whatever you're getting out, leave it! It's not worth it! Save yourself!"

It wasn't as if the house was burning down. But the ham was not turning out the way it was intended to. She yanked on the oven door and clouds of smoke billowed out. What had made the thing burn? She'd only had it in there a couple of hours or so—it shouldn't even be cooked yet. Myrtle frowned ferociously at the uncooperative ham, pulling it out of the oven and turning off the appliance.

She turned to tell Erma that everything was once again under control and she was sure that Erma had other things to do. Erma, however, was already gone. Myrtle felt a niggling bit of worry that this might mean trouble.

Myrtle studied the ham. Could it be salvaged at all? It looked like that glaze had burned for some reason. What if she cut off the glaze and then sliced the ham up? She hesitantly drew closer to the ham and examined it. It looked pretty dry and smelled smoky. But wasn't there smoked ham, after all? People were always drooling over smoked ham, weren't they?

To her horror, she saw Red burst through her front door with a gaping Erma behind him.

"Mama!" he exclaimed. "Is there a fire in the oven? Get out of the house!"

"There's no fire! Just smoke."

"Where there's smoke, there's usually fire," said Red, opening up the oven door and peering inside. He coughed. "This smoke can't be good for you, either." He unlatched her windows and pulled them up as high as they would go. "Don't you have a fan somewhere? Maybe we can blow some of the smoke out." He disappeared into the back of her house.

Myrtle looked irritably at Erma. "Did you have to get Red? He already thinks I'm completely incompetent."

Erma said, "Myrtle, you can't play around with fire. Fire is deadly!"

Myrtle glared at her. Next, she'd be told not to play with matches, and that only she could prevent forest fires. Although imagining Erma in a Smoky the Bear outfit was a nice diversion.

But Erma was continuing on with her lecture. "It's dangerous occurrences like these that make retirement home living look so much easier and better."

"Amen to that!" said Red, lugging in a fan and plugging it in. "What were you doing, Mama?"

"I was cooking a ham for the funeral reception tomorrow," said Myrtle irritably. "I guess some of the glaze must have burned off the bottom of the oven."

Erma peered at the ham. "No, it looks like the glaze *on* the ham burned. It should only be on there for like fifteen minutes or so. How long did you have it in the oven?"

Myrtle paused. "Fifteen minutes."

"No way," said Red, scrutinizing the ham as if trying to do a forensic investigation on it. "That ham was in there for at least an hour or more. It's totally desiccated."

"I'm sure it was fifteen minutes," said Myrtle. She was blessed with the ability to fib convincingly.

Erma was shaking her head, though. "You were in Miles's house for at least an hour, Myrtle. Maybe two hours. Although, I know you lose track of time when you're visiting with him...maybe to you, it didn't seem that long."

Myrtle rolled her eyes and Red seemed to be hiding a smile.

"Well, at any rate, your ham is toast, Mama. You better be thinking of other options for your reception."

Myrtle sniffed. "This ham will work out just fine. It's perfectly smoked. I'll just cut off the glazed area and serve up the ham in biscuits. With plenty of spicy mustard."

"I don't care how much spicy mustard you put on those ham biscuits, Mama, they're still going to be totally dried out," said Red.

"Maybe you could use it like bacon," said Erma, giving her hee-hawing laugh. "It might be about that crunchy."

"Here, Mama, let's just throw it out. Then you can think of something else for this reception." Red opened up her fridge and looked inside. "Looks like you've got a real nice variety of extra-sharp cheese in here."

"It was triple-coupon day," said Myrtle.

"You could slice that up real nice and put some crackers out and that would be one thing you could serve up. I'm sure the church ladies are going to be bringing plenty of food anyway," said Red.

Myrtle carefully put on some oven mitts and picked up the ham. She got out a roll of aluminum foil and wrapped it up with great care, then put it in her fridge. Red and Erma watched her. Red shook his head.

"I think," said Myrtle, "that serving cheese and crackers is just fine for a bunko game or for a children's party. But I'm pretty sure that ham is an absolute requirement for funeral receptions around here. I'll just hold onto that ham and it'll be fine—you'll see."

"As the town's police chief, I won't be party to you killing half the town at a reception. If you want to have somebody make some ham biscuits, I'm sure Elaine wouldn't mind at all if you just watched Jack for her while she's in the kitchen. Or Puddin could make them."

"Puddin!" Myrtle spat out the word as if it was sour.

"Sure," said Red, raising his eyebrows. "Haven't you heard that Puddin is a fine Southern cook? People talk about her all the time. They even get her to cater some of their parties."

Myrtle wasn't sure if it were more irritating that Puddin had never mentioned that she could cook or that Puddin was at the beach and completely inaccessible.

"Puddin is out of town," she said. She hesitated. "Do you think Elaine would mind helping me out?"

Red slumped in relief. "Anything so you won't serve that ham tomorrow."

"I'll probably give some to Pasha. For a treat."

Red shook his head. "I thought you liked that cat, Mama. Don't give it the charcoal ham. I'll talk to Elaine, but I can't imagine there's a problem."

Erma, who'd been gaping at them both in her usual slack-jawed stance, jumped. "Forgot I've got to run to the drugstore to get my prescription for my toe fungus." She bolted out as Myrtle shuddered.

Red seemed distracted still, which always meant it was a good time to ask questions. "How is the case coming along? Have you determined any serious suspects yet?"

Stooping to fan out the oven's interior with a cutting board, Red said absently, "We have a few. Charles Clayborne might not have lived in Bradley, but he sure knew how to make enemies fast."

Myrtle decided it would be safer to affect a lack of curiosity and to repeat what Red already knew that she knew. "That poker player? Seems like he sure made him mad."

"Yes, Lee for one. Apparently, that Charles was something of a slick character and that extended into playing cards. I think the guy was a hustler—trying to wheel and deal and cheat and get money any way he could. I know he's Miles's cousin and all, but he wasn't a great guy," said Red.

"Don't worry about offending Miles. He couldn't stand the man and isn't fond of his mother, either," said Myrtle.

"Yeah, I can understand that. I had to talk to Connie Clayborne for a while and couldn't wait to escape. She kept cooing over her lost boy and trying to show me pictures and talk about what a fine, upstanding young man he was. It was all complete hooey, you could tell. I couldn't decide if she was trying to convince me, or trying to convince herself how perfect that son of hers was."

"So, I'm taking it that he upset other people in town, too?" Myrtle used an offhanded tone. She wanted to know what Red knew without making him suddenly clam up. The high-pressure approach definitely didn't work with him.

"He came in like gangbusters, that's for sure. He was trying to sell something—some kind of fraud or pyramid scheme. Maybe somebody took the bait; then they had second thoughts and he wouldn't give them their money back. Then he was after somebody's wife and the husband wasn't happy about it. Who knows what else he was up to?" Red shook his head. "It's a good thing he got murdered because I'd have had to hire more cops if he'd stayed in town. He was a one-man crime wave, just waiting to happen."

It sounded as if he didn't know anything about Myrtle's dentist's dealings with Charles. Unless, of course, the dentist had been the one who'd wanted his money back. But Dr. Bass sure appeared to have plenty of money and plenty of common sense—it was hard to believe he'd have been taken in on a pyramid scheme.

"How's Elaine's new hobby going?" asked Myrtle with a smile.

Red relaxed, putting the cutting board back and closing the oven door. "You know, this hobby isn't so bad. With digital photography, she just prints out the pictures that are good. It's real forgiving for beginners. It's not as bad as when she was painting, and her paints and canvasses were strewn all over the house.

And bad artwork was all over the house, too— artwork that Red and Myrtle had felt pressured to praise. They exchanged a knowing look with each other.

"She's real motivated with her photography," said Red, looking proud. "Elaine even took Jack with her the other day and took some pictures downtown. And she told me that Sloan Jones is talking about using her pictures at the paper. That inspired her to take on even more."

"Good for her!" said Myrtle. "I'll...uh...well, I'll give her a call shortly. About the ham biscuits." And to remind her to take those zoomed-in pictures at the funeral, just in case Myrtle missed anything.

The problem, decided Myrtle, with a violent death in a small town was that everyone showed up for the funeral. She was sure that most of the people there at the graveside service didn't know Charles Clayborne from a squirrel. They were there to be nosy and find out more details on the murder. Unfortunately, the person they wanted to get that information from was Myrtle.

"Was it awful?" asked one woman in a low voice. "Can you even sleep at night, knowing there was a dead body in your yard? It gives me the willies just thinking about it!"

Her friend nodded and several other people gathered around to hear what Myrtle would say. Although sometimes she didn't mind being the center of attention, this time she was effectively blocked from being able to see what was going on around her and she wanted to hear the post-funeral service hushed chatting.

"No," she said. "Dead bodies don't keep me awake at night. Although the fact that there's a murderer on the loose gives me some sleepless hours. It should for y'all, too. Now, if you'll excuse me...."

Somehow, no one took the hint.

"What did you do when you saw him out there in your yard?" asked another woman. "Did you holler? I'd have just hollered until the police showed up."

Red was standing a couple of yards away from her and shooting her an amused look at her mounting frustration. Obviously, he was doing a better job scanning the crowd for suspicious-looking people than she was. And Lieutenant Perkins from the state police was on the other side of the gathering, watching everyone from the opposite direction.

Things went from bad to worse when Erma Sherman showed up again. "Did y'all know that Myrtle is hosting the funeral reception?" she brayed to the group. "Isn't that nice! I'm going around making sure that everyone knows."

Everyone? But the whole town of Bradley was there! She only wanted the people who were close to Charles to show up. She needed suspects, not every nosy citizen in town.

The service itself had been a bust as far as information went. Connie sat in dignified silence through the short service. She refrained from completely breaking down and from sharing photos from her purse with the other people under the funeral home's tent. Miles had reluctantly taken a seat next to his aunt, at her insistence. The people who didn't realize that Miles was somehow connected to Charles and Connie raised their eyebrows. Other than that, there hadn't been anything particularly interesting. She'd hoped that her dentist, Dr. Bass, would have been there, but he was nowhere in sight, nor was Lee Woosley. So that made two of her suspects that weren't even in attendance.

Right before the funeral ended, she did catch a glimpse of Annette Dawson there—the nurse that Charles was supposedly dallying with shortly after he came to town. Annette actually appeared more upset than even Connie did. Her eye makeup was smeared in big circles on her face, and she kept trying to remove it with a tissue before crying again and making even more mascara run down her face. Tongues really would be wagging. Half the funeral-goers were watching Annette's display of unrequited love as if it were a real-life soap opera.

Another person who acted particularly upset was Lee Woosley's daughter, Peggy Neighbors. Myrtle raised her eyebrows at that. Hadn't Lee told her that Peggy was starting to date Dr. Bass? Why was she so upset about Charles Clayborne's death?

But as soon as the service was over, Myrtle became the attraction, much to her annoyance. Whatever else interesting that was taking place, was happening outside the sphere of the gaggle of busybodies that were crowding around her.

"I've got to get back home and put the food out," she said quickly, before someone else could fit in a question. She grasped her cane, half-seriously considering beating her way out of the gawking gaggle with the stick. Fortunately, the crowd parted before her and she was able to make her way out of the cemetery.

Elaine was her ride. Myrtle yanked open the passenger door on the aging van and climbed in with relief. "Cackling hens," she muttered.

Elaine still had her camera carefully trained on the funeral-goers, clicking down the shutter regularly. "Hmm?" she asked.

"Nothing. Just the typical mob of old ladies that you'd expect to see at any gathering in Bradley. I couldn't get away from them!" said Myrtle. She turned and looked into the backseat, beaming at her grandson. "Hey there, Jack! We had a good time playing this morning, didn't we?"

Elaine said, "Jack told me that y'all played trucks while I put the ham biscuits together. I'm amazed you were able to get off the floor if he had you rolling toys around for over an hour. I know I usually have to pull myself up with the coffee table."

"Oh, these were special trucks," said Myrtle. "Off-road trucks. They had the ability to drive up and down the sofa."

"Smart!" said Elaine. "I'll have to remember to resurrect them the next time I play with him."

"Thanks again for doing those biscuits," said Myrtle with a grimace. "I'd probably have been run out of town on a rail if I hadn't had ham biscuits. Who knew how wild this town was about ham at funerals?"

"It was no problem at all," said Elaine. "I meant to cook something for Miles anyway, so maybe this can be from both of us."

"Did you get any interesting pictures?" asked Myrtle. "What did you see?"

Elaine put the camera down and started up the car. "You know, I'm not real sure what I got. I mostly took crowd shots. So we might have to crop the pictures later to zoom in. I took a few pictures of Annette Dawson, mostly because I couldn't figure out why she was so upset about Charles's death."

"Oh, they were having some kind of fling or something," said Myrtle carelessly.

Elaine gave her a startled look. "How do you always know what's going on?"

"I've got my sources," said Myrtle. "So was there anything else? I was hoping you got something good, because I got waylaid by all the old ladies at the end of the funeral and couldn't see what was going on."

"You know, I did get one interesting thing," said Elaine slowly. "There was this strange-looking woman there. And she was watching the proceedings with this amazing focus. I swear, it was like her eyes were burning through people."

Another suspect? Myrtle's heart beat faster. "What made her strange-looking? What did she look like?"

"She was super-thin and kind of raggedy-looking. I've never seen anything like her. I don't think she had all her teeth, either. Her skin was sort of yellow. I could tell that Red had his eye on her, too."

Myrtle sighed. "Oh, that's just Wanda. You know—that psychic out on the old highway heading out of town. She's a relative of Charles's and I guess she's showing her respects."

"A relative!" Elaine pulled into Myrtle's driveway and stopped to stare at her. "Then she's related to Miles, too. I don't think I've ever seen anybody so different."

"I wonder if she's going to the reception," said Myrtle with a sigh. It was a gloomy prospect. "Oh well. I'll be busy trying to figure out who seems particularly suspicious. Hopefully the murderer will come by my house."

"If anybody else had said that, I'd have thought they were crazy. But coming from you, Myrtle, it almost makes sense. By the way, I put the ham biscuits in your fridge. You know I'd join you, but I think Jack is about ready for some quiet time. I'll catch up with you later, and see how everything is going."

Myrtle bustled around for a few minutes, making sure her tiny hall bathroom was clean, that the kitchen was picked up, and that the food was put out. She'd barely set out everything when there was a tap on her door. Myrtle opened it and saw what looked like most of the town of Bradley out there.

Erma Sherman was leading the pack. "Did you know this many people were going to want to come by and pay their respects?" she asked with a grin as she pushed her way through the door.

"After you announced it all over the funeral I had my suspicions," said Myrtle with a glare that went completely unnoticed.

The line of people stretched from her dining room table all the way down her front walk to the street. She had the feeling that by the time the people on the street came up to the table, there wouldn't even be crumbs left. It all made her feel very grouchy.

Red, despite saying that he wasn't coming to the reception, spent a few minutes there with Lieutenant Perkins from the state police. "Mama," he said, under his breath. "What are all these people doing here? Do you have an open bar or something?"

"Miss Loudmouth Erma blabbed to everyone at the service that I was hosting the reception at my house. I guess they all wanted some free food," grumbled Myrtle.

"I thought people in this town would have realized by now that you're not exactly the Julia Child of Bradley, North Carolina," said Red. "I guess they think that all grandmas are fantastic cooks."

Now she was ready for Red to go back home. Fortunately, he did because she didn't have a clever rejoinder this time—the ham incident had left her with a lack of ammunition.

The problem with having so many people in her small house (well, one of the problems) is that it was hard to keep track of them all. She watched the people waiting outside to come in. They appeared to be quite fascinated by her gnome collection. If only her Viking gnome were still in the backyard!

Connie had been late leaving the cemetery and was one of the last people to arrive. As soon as she saw the unpleasant woman, Myrtle quickly made her way outside to usher her in. Someone like Connie could be useful for uncovering suspects. She was so full of praise for her murdered son, that a suspect's face would likely show extreme distaste while she cooed over Charles.

"I thought the service went very well," said Myrtle, unsure how to compliment a funeral.

Connie nodded tearfully, then looked around her at the crowd of people. "Isn't it such a wonderful tribute? So many people came out to honor Charles's memory. It really speaks to the kind of man he was."

Myrtle had a suspicion that it had more to do with free food.

Once Connie was settled on Myrtle's sofa and someone was dispatched to bring her a plate of food, Myrtle was ready to move closer to her kitchen to see if anyone was looking with diabolical interest at the little memorial she'd made.

She was waylaid en-route. "Myrtle!" crowed old Mrs. Babbitt, clutching her arm with her talon-like hands. "These ham sandwiches are absolutely delightful! Who made them for you?"

Mrs. Babbitt and her friend, Mrs. Cromley, waited with avid interest for her answer. They'd been on various church committees with her for years and apparently thought Myrtle wasn't much of a cook.

"I made them. Every last one of them," she said firmly.

Myrtle suddenly felt as if she was being watched. She turned to see Wanda behind her. The psychic had heard her claim to the ham and she raised her eyebrows and shook her head.

It was all very irritating. Especially since she didn't seem to be getting any compliments on the other food she set out. And the church ladies' food was all gone and only hers remained.

She couldn't seem to go more than two steps without stopping. People were crowded into every square inch of her house. Bradley, North Carolina, was a tiny town—but when it was all gathered in one place, it sure seemed like a mob.

Myrtle heard an angry male voice behind her, but it took nearly a full minute for her to change direction to see who was talking and to whom. It was Silas Dawson, who was not dressed like someone who planned on attending a funeral. He wore what looked like yard clothes, complete with grass stains, and looked as if he hadn't yet shaved. He was totally focused on his wife's face. Annette, the nurse with whom Charles was supposedly having the affair, was still as teary-eyed as she'd been at the funeral service. She had her hands on her hips and her temper appeared to be rising.

"What are you doing here? Don't you know the whole town is staring at you and laughing at me? The guy is dead and your affair with him was over even before he was dead—there's no point coming here and making a fool of both of us in front of everybody," he said, eyes narrowed.

"There is too a point," Annette said, raising her chin stubbornly. "I'm paying my respects. Whether you like it or not, Silas, I had feelings for Charles."

Silas gave a bitter laugh. "Feelings for him? For that guy? What are you thinking—that if he'd lived that y'all would have gotten married and had some happy little life somewhere? Wake up, Annette. He was just looking for a good time. Charles Clayborne would have dumped you in another couple of weeks if he hadn't been murdered first."

"What do you know?" hissed Annette. "Why don't you get out of here? You're the one who's calling attention to yourself, not me. You just stormed in here with your yard clothes on and started hollering at me. If you're so keen to keep a low profile, why don't you just leave? I'll join you back home once I've finished paying my respects."

Silas's gaze darted around the room as she spoke until it rested on Myrtle, who held it. He flushed angrily, turned, and stomped out of the house, pushing people out of his way as he went.

Myrtle turned back around to continue her trek to the kitchen and bumped right into Miles. He had a long-suffering expression on his face. "Really, Myrtle, sometimes you go too far."

She was still thinking about the scene she'd just witnessed between Silas and Annette. "Hmm? Oh, you mean the big spread of food? Well, I wanted to make sure that there was plenty to eat here. Although I'm thinking there won't be. Did you see that the line goes all the way down my front walk to the street? I may have to pop some popcorn."

They both turned and looked out the front door, which was wide open to accommodate the crowd of people. There was still a long line to the street with some people now perching on top of her yard gnomes to rest while they waited, feet and legs engulfed by the tall grass.

Myrtle frowned. "Some of those folks look a little heavy to be sitting on my gnomes. I hope they won't hurt them. I've already had one gnome carted off by the forensic team and I don't want to lose any more."

"No, Myrtle, I'm not talking about the food. I'm talking about your little memorial out in your backyard," said Miles.

"What about it? I told you I was going to do it as a focal point for the reception." She lowered her voice. "I was going to watch people's reaction to it. Except there are so many blasted people here that I can't even get to the kitchen to observe anything."

"Yes, you told me you were making a small memorial. But I thought you were going to do something tasteful," said Miles.

Myrtle blinked at him. "I did do something tasteful, Miles. What are you talking about?"

"I'm talking about what you did out there. It's *not* tasteful, Myrtle. I'm not sure what alternate universe it would be considered tasteful in, but it's not this one. I'm just hoping my aunt doesn't see it or she'll start making a scene." Miles grimaced at the thought.

"What's not tasteful about a few flowers scattered on the ground?" Myrtle put her hands on her hips, bumping a few people with her elbows as she did.

"Flowers? Well, I *guess* there were flowers out there. It was kind of hard to see them considering the reenactment you created," said Miles.

"Reenactment? What?"

Miles sighed. "The body. The body that you put out there as a reenactment. At least, that's what I've been telling everybody who's asked me about it. Sounds better than to explain that you've clearly lost your mind."

Myrtle grew very still. "But Miles. I didn't put a body out there. Not for a reenactment. Not for any reason. I only put a few flowers out there."

Chapter Ten

Miles and Myrtle stared at each other.

"You didn't stuff a man's suit and put a dummy out there?" asked Miles in an unsteady voice.

Myrtle shook her head.

"You didn't ask someone to volunteer to be a body in order to reenact the tragic evening Cousin Charles died?"

Myrtle shook her head.

Miles took a deep breath. "Then this reception is over. I'll go get Red. You make sure that nobody goes out there and messes with the crime scene."

He dashed out the front door—it was more of a twisting, turning, pushing type of dodging dash—and Myrtle stepped outside into the backyard, closing the door behind her. She wouldn't dream of tampering with the crime scene (well, not this time, anyway), but she did want to take a closer look at it.

It was Lee Woosley, her handyman. It looked as if he wouldn't be finishing those projects for her after all. He appeared to have been struck on the back of the head with the shovel that Dusty had forgotten and had fallen face first—apparently on top of her memorial. How anyone thought this could be a reenactment of Charles's murder was inconceivable. This time, there was no Viking gnome in evidence for one thing.

What had he been doing in Myrtle's backyard? What had the murderer been doing in Myrtle's backyard—again? And how could Myrtle continue missing the most excitement her yard had seen since Red and his buddies played kickball there?

Red would be over in seconds and he would be coming around the side of the house, not bothering with pushing his way through the crowded house. She stooped and squinted at the ground. There was no sign of any footprints in the dry soil. There hadn't been anything left behind by the killer that she could see. A wallet with ID surely would have been helpful. Lee didn't seem to be clutching a note with a scrawled meeting time on it—that would have been helpful, too.

But it did appear that Lee had been planning on going to either the funeral or the reception, or both. He was not in his usual handyman clothing, but wore slacks and a button-down shirt. He looked to be lying mostly on top of something. Myrtle peered closer and saw that it was a small toolbox—not the big one he'd brought when he came over to do her repairs. And there *was* something just barely visible in one hand. She stooped, then stood back up. Screws. Lee had come back over to fix her planter so everything would be perfect before the funeral reception.

Myrtle put her hands innocently behind her back as she heard heavy breathing coming around the side of her house. Moments later, Red appeared looking flushed and annoyed. Miles was right behind him.

They gazed silently at the dead man.

"Right on top of my memorial," said Myrtle after a moment.

"Mama, don't you think this is getting extreme? Two bodies in your yard? This time you even have a house full of guests."

"Well, it's not like I'm responsible for this, Red. If I were, I'd certainly have chosen a different time of day for a body to appear in my backyard. Preferably one when I'm around to look out the window and catch the murderer." Myrtle was very cross at her failure to observe murder mere yards from her. "It looks like Lee came back with the right screws or bolts to hang my planter back on the wall."

They continued looking at Lee. Miles cleared his throat. "Not to be pushy, but what are we going to do about the funeral reception. I feel mildly responsible for the guests, considering my connection to the first victim."

Red rubbed the side of his face. "I've got to call Lieutenant Perkins and tell him we've got another body. They'll need to get the forensics team over here. I should talk to the guests before they go and find out if anyone saw anything. Although I'm guessing that this murder took place while the funeral was going on."

Suddenly, panicked screaming cut off Red's calm instructions. She could hear Pasha growling and hissing inside. Myrtle yanked the back-door open and saw Pasha launching herself at a shrieking Erma Sherman. "Get it off me!" she hollered.

"Leave Pasha alone," said Myrtle in her old schoolteacher's voice. She held out her arms and Erma peeled off the cat and tossed it at her. Myrtle crooned to Pasha softly.

"Whut're you going to do?" grated a ruined voice behind her and Myrtle turned around to see Wanda.

"About what?" asked Myrtle. But she had a feeling that the psychic knew.

Wanda knitted her brows, looking impatient. "About the body. There's about to be a scene. Ain't the cop going to get us out of the house? It's too crowded. Going to be a lot of pushing and shoving when the scene starts."

Myrtle frowned at Wanda. "How do you know there's about to be a scene?"

Wanda looked mysterious. "Might want to put the cat down."

Clearly, she couldn't put it outside in the crime scene. Myrtle el-bowed her way to her bedroom and shut the cat in there, hearing Red's voice calmly asking everyone to file out in an orderly fashion and line up on the sidewalk.

More screaming cut off Red's calm instructions. She could hear Pasha growling and hissing from her bedroom, and was glad Wanda had given her a heads-up. She craned her neck to see who was making all the racket this time.

Unfortunately, it was Peggy Neighbors—Lee Woosley's daughter. Myrtle hadn't seen her and obviously Red hadn't either, or else he'd have ushered her off to the side first.

"Daddy!" she gasped, propping herself up on the back windowsill as if not trusting herself to stand up.

Everyone gaped at her, and then moved, almost as one entity, to peer through the window into Myrtle's ill-fated backyard. The mutterings got louder and louder.

Red re-established control with a roar. "Everyone out the *front* door *now*! To the front sidewalk and wait. Now!"

It quickly became quiet, and they all filed out into the front yard. Miles trailed behind.

Myrtle assumed that Red didn't include poor Peggy in his order. Or his mother. After all, she was an octogenarian, for heaven's sake—it was ridiculous for her to stand outside on a blazing sidewalk in the full sun after such an exhausting and stressful day. So she stayed inside and walked quietly over to Peggy, putting an arm around her as they both looked out the window.

"I'm so sorry, Peggy. Your father was a fine man. He actually was over here helping me out with some repairs just a few days ago."

Peggy sniffed and Myrtle quickly reached for a nearby tissue box. Finally, Peggy said in a small voice, "Now I've lost both parents. It's just my daughter and me now. And I just don't understand at all. Why would somebody kill Daddy? Over here? What could have happened?"

Since Peggy seemed to be trying to work it all out in her head, Myrtle was happy to think it through with her. Particularly, since Red would be sure to cut their conversation short as soon as he realized she wasn't outside.

"Peggy, did you talk to your dad at all today? Was he at the funeral?" She hadn't seen him there, but maybe she'd just missed him.

Peggy gulped and struggled to contain her emotions. "I talked to him for only a minute or two this morning. He said he might not make it to the funeral because there was something he had to do for work." She stopped, and a horrified look crossed her face. "And we were arguing. Oh no! Our last conversation was an argument."

"Honey, it happens," said Myrtle quietly.

"He said he wasn't going to the funeral, but that he'd be at the reception afterwards." She looked up at Myrtle. "Do you think that maybe he was here to finish up part of the job he'd done?"

Myrtle said slowly, "I do think he was here to finish the job, yes. The only thing he hadn't done was hang my planter back up on the wall for me. It looked like he'd come back with the right screws to mount it." She paused. "Was your dad having a problem with anyone? Arguments? Disagreements?"

Peggy shook her head vehemently. "Absolutely not. Everybody loved him."

Myrtle hesitated. "But Red told me that your dad had an argument with Charles Clayborne before he died."

Now Peggy looked evasive. "Charles Clayborne?" she asked, as if not remembering the name.

"Yes. The man whose funeral this is," said Myrtle patiently. There had to be something there. Why was Peggy acting as if she and her father didn't know Charles?

Peggy quickly said, "Of course. Silly of me. I guess it's the shock. Yes, Daddy had an argument with him because he thought Charles was cheating him at poker. Other than that, I can't think of any problems he's had with anybody."

Myrtle could hear Red's voice near her front door. Shoot. He was coming too quickly. "Did you see your dad at the reception when you got here?"

Peggy shook her head solemnly. "I sure didn't. I was looking for him too—to apologize for the way I'd spoken to him on the phone this morning." Her voice started shaking again as she thought about their argument.

"What was it that you were arguing about this morning?" asked Myrtle as Red came hurrying through the front door, calling her name. "That is," she added quickly, "I'm sure that it couldn't have been as bad as you're thinking, Peggy."

"It *was* bad," said Peggy, but stopped talking as Red came up to them.

"Mama, I thought I told you to come outside." Red's voice was tight with stress.

"I figured you'd want me to stay with Peggy," said Myrtle coolly. "Surely you didn't intend for her to be standing in the front yard with all the gaping masses."

"Is it all right if I use your bathroom?" asked Peggy.

"Of course. Right down the hall. And there are clean washcloths under the sink if you want to refresh yourself a little. It's been such a shock, I know."

"Do you have an aspirin or something?" she asked, pressing her fingers against her forehead.

"Right in the medicine cabinet," said Myrtle as Peggy walked out of the room.

Red gave her a stern look.

"Well, what was I supposed to do?" Myrtle asked with a shrug.

"Has it occurred to you that there appears to be a murderer hanging out at your house?" asked Red in a hushed voice. "Maybe it would be a good idea if you stuck close to me."

Myrtle put her hands on her hips. "Where exactly would this murderer be hiding in my house? Hmm? This isn't exactly a mansion, Red."

"Under your bed."

"He'd have to push aside fifteen different boxes to hide under there. It just wouldn't be an efficient place for a murderer to hide," said Myrtle.

"While Peggy is in the bathroom, why don't you fill me in? What did Peggy tell you?" asked Red. "Did she say anything about what might have happened?"

Myrtle reluctantly filled him in with what she knew.

Then Peggy came back out and Red said, "Now Mama, I'm going to talk to Peggy for a few minutes. I need for you to go outside and rejoin your guests. Lieutenant Perkins is out there talking to them now. Besides, I think the forensics team might want to be in your house awhile, too."

Not that they were going to get any good clues from the house. Most of the town had been in there, sloppily leaving their DNA around. She grabbed her cane and headed to the front door.

It proved to be more interesting outside than Myrtle had thought. Lieutenant Perkins was busily conducting short interviews with the guests, giving Myrtle time to conduct her own without being frowned at.

She was immediately pounced on outside, as she'd known she would be. First of all, the old McKenzie sisters grabbed her arm.

"Isn't it awful!" one of the elderly sisters said to Myrtle with gleaming eyes. "I simply can't believe it. And isn't this the second time now that you've had a body in your backyard? How terrifying!"

"We all have our own peculiar trials to bear," said Myrtle. She was already pulling away because, if her past dealings with the sisters were any guide, they were heavy on drama and low on real information.

The older of the sisters dug her claw-like nails into Myrtle's arm a little more, apparently for support since she wavered a bit on her feet.

"I saw it, you know. I saw the body." A satisfied expression crossed her face.

"I think most of the party saw it," said Myrtle impatiently. "And, technically, I believe we should be referring to the body as *him*."

"I mean, I saw **him** *before* everyone realized it was real," said the woman in an insistent voice. Once she saw she had Myrtle's attention, she continued. "I got to your house right after you did," she said to Myrtle.

"We'd heard you had an open bar," her sister helpfully interjected.

"Erroneously, clearly," said the older sister, her voice heavy with disapproval.

So that's why the attendance at the reception had been so heavy. It hadn't all been Erma Sherman's fault. Unless she'd been the one behind the rumor.

"When I came in your house, I looked around a bit. To get my bearings, you know. Find where the sandwiches were; find where the powder room was...."

"And figure out where the drinks table was," said the younger sister with a disappointed sigh.

"When I looked outside—just wondering, of course, if there were possibly some additional refreshments outside—I thought that you'd had a fairly uncharacteristic lapse of good taste. We've all gotten used to small memorials, of course. We see teddy bears, balloons, flowers and flags all the time to commemorate an untimely death. But using a manikin to depict a reenactment of the scene—well, it seemed to me that Myrtle Clover had gone too far. You do remember my saying that, don't you, Sister?"

"I certainly do, Sister. I certainly do!"

Myrtle said, "All right, just summing up this story of yours, you're saying that you were one of the first guests at my reception and you noticed that there was already a body in the backyard when you arrived?"

The elderly woman's thin face beamed at her. "That's right!" She paused. "Is that important, do you think? Do you think the policeman will be interested?"

"I think it helps to pinpoint the time of death," said Myrtle, finally managing to pull her arm away from the woman's digging fingers. "I was starting to wonder if it had happened during the reception itself. Everyone was so distracted stuffing themselves with ham sandwiches...."

"And looking for the bar," reminded the younger sister.

"...that I wondered if a murder might have taken place in full view of everyone and nobody even noticed," finished Myrtle. "But it sounds like that wasn't true."

"What I'd like to know, though," said the older sister with avid interest, "is more about how you discovered the very first body. Who exactly was this Charles Clayborne? And what on earth was he doing lying dead in your yard?"

Myrtle gave her best impression of a regretful smile. "I'd love to be able to share that information with you, but it's classified. Besides," she said, catching sight of Wanda staring at her from a few yards away, "there's someone that I need to talk to."

"Thanks for giving me that warning about putting Pasha down," said Myrtle. "She'd have carved me up into a million pieces with those claws when all the screaming started up."

Wanda nodded and smiled, looking down somewhere in the direction of her scruffy shoes. Shyness from the psychic? It had to be due to her being out of her comfort zone.

Myrtle continued. "So you knew? You'd seen the body out the window before you warned me?"

Wanda shrugged an emaciated shoulder. "Seen it in my head."

Was Myrtle ever going to get used to this hocus-pocus stuff? "If you saw the death before it happened, why didn't you let the police know? Red would've...."

Wanda gave a scornful snort. "Red would've patted me on the back and sent me off. Would've thought I was crazy or making stuff up."

He would have, at that.

"Besides, ain't seen details. I thought I was seeing the *other* body again. Like a rerun. Didn't know it was a fresh body," said Wanda.

Myrtle glanced around to make sure no one was in earshot, then said in a low voice, "Tell me who you favor for the murderer. Have you seen anything in your head about how these murders happened? Any shadowy figures? People lurking in my bushes? A hint as to who did it?"

Wanda shook her head. "Wish I did. But there's nothing."

"All right. But you seem like a pretty perceptive person." An understatement. "You were at the reception and might have gotten more of a chance to watch people than I did. Did you pick up on anything? See anybody acting suspicious? Hear any threads of conversation that might give us a clue as to who's behind all this?" asked Myrtle.

Wanda looked at Myrtle shrewdly. "Yer in danger."

Chapter Eleven

Not this again. "I know. But if I find out who's responsible for these killings, then I won't be in danger anymore, will I? Can't you help me out?"

The appeal seemed to sway the woman. She sighed. "Don't know if it's important. But that Peggy? She had a past with that Charles."

"Charles Clayborne? Your cousin? She used to be involved with him romantically, you're saying?" asked Myrtle. She remembered seeing Peggy crying at Charles's funeral.

"Used to be. Still wanted to be," said Wanda coolly.

"But she was practically telling me she didn't know who Charles even was!"

"Came to his funeral, didn't she?" asked Wanda. "Cried over his body, too."

That she had. "And you're saying that she still wanted to get back together with Charles?" The two seemed like an odd match to Myrtle. Charles, slick as he was, was still a fairly attractive man. Peggy was pleasantly plump and looked older than her thirty-six years.

Wanda nodded. "That's what I heard. She was trying to hitch back up with him and he wasn't wanting to. Hurt her feelings."

Hurt feelings were understandable. But would that be enough to kill someone? And she certainly hadn't appeared to know anything about her father's death. It was hard to picture Peggy being responsible for killing her own father. Could there possibly be more than one murderer afoot?

Her thoughts were interrupted by Lieutenant Perkins. "Mrs. Clover? Could I speak with you for a few minutes?" Myrtle had forgotten that she was probably a person of interest to the state police. How many times could you have a body in your backyard without attracting attention?

They stepped off to the side and the sergeant with Lieutenant Perkins flipped to a fresh page in his notebook and looked at Myrtle expectantly. He had such an eager expression on his face that she felt sorry to have to dash his hopes.

Which she did almost immediately. "Lieutenant Perkins, I would love to be able to help you out. But I'm like the little monkeys who saw and heard no evil. I'm completely useless to you. As far as I can tell, I had a body in my backyard for hours and had absolutely no idea that it was there."

Lieutenant Perkins retained his same thoughtful expression, but she did see the sergeant's face fall.

Perkins said, "So when you returned from the funeral service, you didn't notice there was another victim in your yard?"

"No. Wish I had, though." Myrtle could tell her irritation at that fact was seeping into her voice.

"There appeared to be a small memorial set out in the yard that was directly under the victim. Could you give me an idea when you set that out?" asked the police officer.

"It's probably not going to help you out much. I put those flowers out there early this morning; right after the sun came up. Clearly he was murdered sometime after the flowers were placed outside, but I already knew that he was still alive this morning." Myrtle abruptly slammed her mouth closed. He wouldn't have spoken to Peggy Neighbors yet, and if she filled him in, it was going to make her look nosy again. The police warnings did wear thin after a while.

But her comment hadn't escaped notice. "How did you know that Lee Woosley was still alive this morning?" he asked. The sergeant was beginning to look excited again and had his pencil poised once more over the notebook.

Myrtle sighed. "Lee's daughter, Peggy Neighbors, talked to him on the phone this morning. She told me about it a few minutes ago."

As expected, Lieutenant Perkins gave Myrtle a disapproving look. Before he could offer her his standard police warning, Myrtle decided that the interview was entirely too one-sided and that she needed to turn the tables. "It looked like someone had smacked Lee on the back of the head with a shovel—is that right? Could a woman have done it?"

Perkins seemed to be mulling over how much to disclose.

Myrtle said, "Don't you think you could share just a tad bit of information with me? These murders are happening directly in my yard. If I know what you know, maybe I can avoid being the next victim. Knowledge is power, after all."

"In some situations, maybe," he answered finally. "I can't think how it might help you in this one. But I can confirm that the blow with the shovel killed Lee Woosley nearly instantly. It looks like he was probably killed during the funeral service while he was about to finish some home repairs for you. It's likely that he never saw his murderer."

It sure wasn't much to go on. She'd learned more from talking with Wanda.

"What about Charles Clayborne's death?" she asked. "Have you found out any more about it?"

"Only that the murder probably occurred somewhere around ten-thirty," said Perkins, coolly. "And that unfortunately, none of the neighbors heard anything. You've said you were showering around that time. And apparently your cat was upset and they turned on various noise-making devices to drown out the cat."

"Pasha was probably trying to protect me by giving an alarm," said Myrtle. "The feral, furry love."

"And now, Mrs. Clover," said the detective smoothly, "I suggest that you keep out of this investigation. There's a very dangerous person on the loose and he appears to be sticking very close to your home. If he thinks you're learning too much about his identity...." He trailed off suggestively.

"My concern is simply staying safe, Lieutenant," Myrtle said quickly. And it was—it just wasn't her *only* concern. She saw Miles sternly watching her from several yards away. He was always able to read her mind.

It felt like a long time before she was able to go back to her house. When she finally got inside, she let Pasha out. (The cat gave her a very reproachful look as she did.) Plopping down on her sofa, Myrtle realized she was worn absolutely slap-out. She wasn't sure whether her exhaustion was due more to the appearance of a second body in her backyard, or the stress of hosting a funeral reception for what had ended up being the entire town.

When her doorbell rang, she was very tempted to just turn the volume of her soap on louder and ignore it. "The food's all gone!" she hollered in case it was a returning guest looking for seconds. "No more ham!"

"I'm glad it was such a success," called Elaine's voice through the front door.

Myrtle decided that Elaine was definitely worth the trip to unlock the door. She received the bonus reward of a visit from her grandson. Jack grinned at her and handed her an ambulance.

"It's Jack's way of saying hi," said Elaine dryly.

"After today, I'll just about need that ambulance," said Myrtle. "Too bad I can't even fit my pinky toe in there."

They settled in the kitchen and Myrtle poured them all lemonades. "I'm surprised that Red is even letting you and Jack in here," said Myrtle. "He was pretty convinced earlier that my house was some kind of death trap with murderers leaping out at every opportunity."

"Oh, well, he doesn't know we're here," said Elaine in a breezy voice as she took a glass of lemonade from Myrtle. "But I can't say that I'm surprised by his thoughts on the matter. Are you sure you don't want to stay with us for a while? Just until the murderer is caught. You'd probably sleep a lot better at night."

"I don't sleep at night as it is," said Myrtle.

"Maybe *I'd* sleep better then," said Elaine.

"Besides," said Myrtle, "Lee Woosley wasn't even murdered at night."

"Even worse," said Elaine. "That means that there's no pattern to his behavior so you're really always in danger here."

"I'm not all that worried about it," said Myrtle. "But I reserve the right to suddenly and irrationally become very concerned about the murderer and take you up on your offer later. In case I think Red is harboring some good information on the case and I want to have more opportunities to squeeze it out of him."

"This time maybe I'm the one with all the information," said Elaine, looking unusually smug.

"Oh right! The pictures from the funeral service," said Myrtle. "I'd almost forgotten about them."

"And not only that, but during Jack's nap I also took my camera out and trained it on all your reception guests as they were waiting to talk to Lieutenant Perkins." Now Elaine was looking seriously pleased with herself.

Myrtle clapped her hands with glee, spurring Jack to stop what he was doing and clap too. Myrtle beamed at him.

"Can I see what you took, Elaine? How many pictures did you take?"

Elaine was peering deeply into her purse, and rummaging for the camera. "Probably around three-hundred. The camera wouldn't hold anymore, actually, and I had to stop shooting."

"Three-*hundred*?" It seemed like an awful lot of pictures, but there were two events, after all...still.

As soon as Myrtle held the camera, she could tell the process of looking through the pictures was going to take a while. Poor Elaine didn't appear to have any kind of internal editor at all. She'd take a picture of just about anything that moved. There also looked to be a whole lot of photos of Elaine's finger. Myrtle suppressed a sigh.

Elaine was still smiling eagerly. "I'm really enjoying this hobby, Myrtle. In fact, I was wondering when I can stop treating it like a hobby and start treating it like a profession. I'm taking pictures for the paper, after all."

Surely, Sloan Jones wasn't going to find time out of his editorial duties to comb through three-hundred bad photos to pick out a couple for his newspaper. And Elaine looked so happy, too.

"The only thing that's really a problem," said Elaine, knitting her brows, "is searching through all the pictures for the perfect shot. Whenever I've sat down to try to do it, Jack has some kind of radar that goes off and makes him need me for something. I've got to get the pictures that I need off the camera, especially since I don't have more room on it to take more."

Myrtle took a deep breath and said, "Would you like me to go through them for you? All I was going to do for the rest of the afternoon was sit in my chair and relax. Might as well look through your pictures. I could jot down the ones on a notepad that look the best. Doesn't each picture have a number assigned to it, or something?"

Elaine frowned with concern. "They do. But you were going to sit in your chair and nap, weren't you? I'm pretty sure your plan for the afternoon didn't involve fishing through photos on a camera. The screen is super small, too."

There was that. "Can't you hook up the camera to my computer or something? You're right—I won't be able to really see anything on that tiny screen."

"But your computer is on your desk. You don't want to sit at your desk for that long, do you?"

Not particularly.

"How about if I bring by my laptop and hook it up to the camera? Then you can sit in your chair and look at the pictures. Then I can go back and make some supper—I think Jack is probably starving. Want me to bring you over some food after I'm done cooking? Then I can pick up the laptop and camera at the same time?" asked Elaine.

Myrtle was about to say no, but then her stomach growled. She remembered that she hadn't even gotten a chance to eat at her own reception. In fact, she hadn't eaten anything since breakfast. Elaine was a great cook. Her tummy growled again.

"I'll take that as a yes," said Elaine with a grin. "And thanks so much, Myrtle. I was starting to wonder if I was going to have to stay up all night, looking at those pictures after Jack had turned in. I know Sloan is ready for them."

Myrtle was ready for them, too.

Once she'd settled into the chore of sorting through the photos, she found that the pictures weren't all as bad as she'd feared. Yes, there were lots of close-ups of Elaine's finger, but did it matter? You could still see most of what she'd been pointing her camera toward.

She'd gotten a nice shot at the funeral service of a tearful Peggy Neighbors—when Peggy had only been upset by Charles Clayborne's death and not her father's. Her picture of Annette Dawson hadn't been as good—too blurry—but you could still see that Annette had a combination of sadness and determination on her face.

There appeared to be quite a few pictures of Myrtle, too, which Myrtle couldn't completely understand. She noticed that she had a fairly nosy look on her face in all the pictures and that her surreptitious glances weren't quite as surreptitious as she'd hoped.

She sighed and continued on. The pictures that Elaine had taken at the beginning of her reception showed a line of bored people waiting to get inside Myrtle's house. As they stayed in line, the pictures showed the guests looking more irritable. Myrtle made a face. Just as well she couldn't hear what they'd been saying. In one of the photos, everyone appeared especially grim, and she marked that one in her notebook as a good one for Sloan. They could just as easily be responding to news of the murder instead of worrying over whether there'd be any food or beverages left.

Elaine had apparently shifted her grip on the camera when Miles came over to report the murder. She had several pictures of her entire palm before finally getting the camera pointed at the people instead.

The people in the photos changed as everyone left the house showing various stages of confusion, panic, and dismay. There was lots of talking in small groups, and watching as the police cars arrived and the forensic team went around to the back of the house. But there was nothing particularly unusual about any of it. Annette Dawson looked shocked, but she'd seemed shocked earlier, too.

There were several pictures of Wanda looking directly at the camera. This, even though Elaine was taking these pictures from inside her house on a bright, sunny day. Myrtle shivered. It was a good thing that Wanda was working for the good guys and not for the forces of evil.

And then Myrtle paused. There was a picture that showed her dentist, Dr. Bass, standing off to the side and looking intently at the proceedings. What was he doing there? He certainly hadn't been at the funeral or the reception.

There was also another picture, clearly taken days earlier, showing the elusive Dr. Bass having a conversation with Lee Woosley outside a downtown barber shop. Dr. Bass had a tired expression on his face.

It was time to find out what exactly Dr. Bass's connection to Charles Clayborne was. And why had he been talking with Lee Woosley, who was now victim number two? Myrtle decided then and there that Miles needed a trip to the dentist. With a supportive friend tagging along.

Chapter Twelve

"What?" Miles looked as though she'd suggested a trip to Mars instead of the dentist.

"I'm proposing that you have a dental cleaning, Miles. Men are notoriously bad at scheduling visits to take care of their health and I'm a concerned friend."

"Or a nosy one," muttered Miles.

"Regardless. When was the last time you had your teeth cleaned, Miles?"

Miles tightened his lips.

"That long, huh? Well, this will be perfect. We'll head over to see Dr. Bass and I'll come along for moral support," said Myrtle.

"My teeth are in wonderful shape. I've never even had a cavity." Miles sounded sullen.

"They certainly won't stay that way for very long if you don't get them cleaned. You're clearly phobic, Miles. It's a good thing that I came along when I did," said Myrtle.

"I have all my own teeth," said Miles, stressing the point.

Myrtle blinked at him. "For heaven's sake. So do I! Just because I'm old doesn't mean I have dentures. How biased of you, Miles." Of course, most of her teeth had fillings in them, but she certainly wasn't going to tell him that. It was all due to the fact that the tap water hadn't had fluoride during her formative years.

Miles groaned. "I can see I'm not getting out of this. I'd rather not see your dentist, though. Don't you suspect him of murder? It seems dumb for me to put myself in harm's way."

"He's an excellent dentist. Besides, he's the only dentist in town."

"I have a car. I could drive to another town to see a dentist elsewhere," said Miles.

"Don't rub in the fact that you still own wheels, Miles. And there's no point in seeing another dentist, because the whole reason we're doing this is to find out what Dr. Bass's connection with Charles Clayborne was."

"I thought the whole reason we were going was out of concern for my dental health," grumbled Miles.

"We're knocking out two birds with one stone," said Myrtle coolly. "Besides, I think you owe me a favor."

"For....?" Miles frowned at her.

"Hosting a lovely reception for your cousin's funeral, of course."

"Was it lovely?" Miles squinted doubtfully at the ceiling. "As I recall, it ended rather abruptly with a dead body on the premises."

"That was, naturally, out of my hands. I had no idea there was a body outside my house," said Myrtle sternly. She pulled a small notebook out of her purse and opened it. "Here's his office number." Myrtle watched as Miles reluctantly walked over to the phone and made the appointment for the next morning.

He sighed as he got off the phone. "Well, that's done. Tell me again why you're suspecting your dentist has something to do with all this?"

"You remember my telling you about Elaine's new hobby, don't you?"

Miles winced. "Yes. How is the hobby du jour going? Have you seen lots of headless people in her pictures?"

"Mostly a lot of close-ups of Elaine's fingers. But I have seen one interesting thing. I've noticed that Dr. Bass keeps popping up in her pictures," said Myrtle. "He was in one of her pictures taken after the sudden ending of my reception."

Miles shrugged. "He's a resident of the town. And the whole town was there. Maybe he just happened to be passing, wondered what was going on, and then decided to stop by."

"I don't think so," said Myrtle. "I think he was lurking there. He had to have known about the funeral reception—the entire town of Bradley knew about it, so why wouldn't he? No, I think he was there for a reason...and I intend to find out why."

Dr. Bass wasn't the one to clean Miles's teeth, of course. It was that hygienist that had been Myrtle's former student. Unfortunately, she appeared to harbor a grudge against Myrtle and it appeared she was taking it out on Miles's teeth. He glared at Myrtle when the cleaning was finally over.

"I'll go get the doctor to check your teeth now," said Pam, sounding surly. Myrtle noticed with satisfaction that the hygienist wasn't calling her sweetheart or hon or darlin' anymore.

Nor, thankfully, did she come back in with Dr. Bass.

Myrtle cleared her throat. "Dr. Bass! What a pleasure to see you again!"

Dr. Bass's brow wrinkled in confusion. "Oh. It's very nice to see you, too, Mrs. Clover," he said pleasantly.

He was now looking at her as if she were a very foggy old woman. This was perfect, since Myrtle was adept at using that to her advantage.

She was going to have to make this snappy, though, getting to the point more directly than she usually did. The dentist's office was packed with patients and Dr. Bass was already giving her impatient looks.

"You know my daughter-in-law Elaine, don't you? Red's wife?"

"Yes, yes, of course I do," Dr. Bass replied in a hurried voice. "Is she doing well?"

"She's just fine. She might need to make an appointment with you, though," said Myrtle thoughtfully. That would be a good way to get back in here, wouldn't it? Myrtle would need to watch Jack, of course, while Elaine got her teeth cleaned. "But what I was going to mention is that she's working for the paper right now. As a photographer. You know how the *Bradley Bugle* loves its human interest stories."

Dr. Bass was signaling for Miles to open his mouth and was pushing a stool over to look inside. "That's very interesting, Mrs. Clover," he said in a distracted voice.

"I thought so, too. I also thought it was interesting that she'd taken a snapshot showing you talking to Charles Clayborne." Myrtle blinked innocently at him. "Elaine was showing me some of her photography and I saw this picture of the two of you talking together downtown. It didn't look like a pleasant conversation, either."

She couldn't have asked for more of a reaction from the dentist. A splotchy red blush started from his white coat all the way up to his red hair. Myrtle got the distinct impression, however, that the ruddiness was due to anger and not embarrassment.

He shrugged and then examined Miles's teeth, apparently trying to collect his thoughts or his emotions or both. "It's a small town. I run into many people on a daily basis."

"Oh, I'm sure that's true. Especially being a dentist. You've probably got most of the town approaching you to tell you all about their tooth pain or the problem with an old filling. But this is different, isn't it? You'd told me just days ago that you hadn't talked to Charles Clayborne in over a decade. And there you were, having a spirited conversation with him in downtown Bradley, shortly before Charles was murdered," said Myrtle with a shrug of her own.

Dr. Bass gave her a sharp look. "I'd forgotten, that's all. And I'm sure it wasn't a spirited conversation; it was probably a very boring one—which explains why I promptly forgot about it."

He looked away from her and back at his patient and Myrtle got that irritated feeling she always got whenever she felt dismissed.

She cleared her throat. "There was one more picture that Elaine snapped. This one showed you talking with Lee Woosley. Actually, it's amazing that Elaine would happen to capture you on film at all—you don't get out much. Anyway—I was wondering what y'all were discussing. You and Lee."

Dr. Bass gazed at her with the same tired look he'd had in the photo Elaine had snapped. "Mrs. Clover, Lee Woosley has been trying to play matchmaker between me and his daughter ever since we were in high school together. I was fielding his latest attempt, that's all."

Myrtle was just opening her mouth to follow up on that statement when Dr. Bass cut her off. "If you'll excuse me, Mrs. Clover, I need to finish up with Mr. Bradford."

Myrtle snapped her mouth shut as Dr. Bass suddenly grew very busy with Miles's x-rays. "Unfortunately, Mr. Bradford, I do see some evidence of tooth decay here. You have a cavity right here." He showed Miles on the x-ray. Miles looked completely horrified.

"Are you sure about that, Dr. Bass? I mean, I'm sure you are. It's just that I've never had a cavity before in my life. And my teeth haven't been bothering me much," said Miles, all in a rush.

"But you don't eat a lot of extremely hot or extremely cold food," said Myrtle knowingly. "You're not an ice cream or a soup eater. You might not have noticed it at all." For some reason, it was giving her great glee that smug Miles was now afflicted with a tooth issue. And the fact that she had been the one to get him to the dentist made her fill with self-righteousness.

"It's a very small cavity, so you might not have been aware that you had a problem," said the dentist mildly. "It's good that you came in as early as you did, though—it won't take much to fix this problem. We'll make a follow-up appointment for you to come back to have the tooth filled."

Myrtle beamed at Miles and was rewarded with a dirty look.

The short car ride home was tense. "All that trouble and you didn't even find out anything," grumbled Miles.

"I did. I found out that Dr. Bass will lie when asked about Charles Clayborne. That says a lot, Miles. It tells us that there's something between Charles and Dr. Bass that he doesn't want anyone to find out about."

"If he's so bound and determined to keep his secret, what makes you so sure you're going to be able to find it out, yourself?" asked Miles. "Are you going to pin him down in his own dental chair and dope him up on gas and give him the third degree?"

Actually, that sounded like a wonderful idea. If only Myrtle were just a few years younger.

"No," she answered briskly, "I'm thinking more that I've got to get this information from someone he knows. In a town like Bradley, *somebody* has to know something. Even if they're the best secret-keeper in the world, if it's a juicy enough secret and they've been hanging onto it for decades...they're about ready to pop. I'm going to figure out who Dr. Bass's friends used to be and who they are now. He won't be keeping his secret for very long."

Myrtle stole a sideways look at Miles. "We also learned something else while we were at the dentist."

"What's that," asked Miles with a long-suffering sigh.

"We learned that you have cavities," said Myrtle, smiling.

Back at home, Myrtle started making her list of people to talk to about Dr. Bass. The man wasn't married, unfortunately, so there was no spouse to contact. The fact that Dr. Bass was unmarried likely accounted for much of his popularity in town—especially among the women. He wasn't a bad-looking man and he was still a relatively young one. At her age, Myrtle considered him a mere infant.

She was drawing a blank, though. What on earth did Dr. Bass do with his free time? Now that she thought about it, she couldn't think of a time when she'd seen him around town. Oh, she'd seen him at the grocery store. But she never saw him walking into town, visiting with people as he went. She never saw him in the park, watching the free movies that aired every Friday night during the summer. He didn't seem to take a boat out on the lake much. Come to think of it, she hadn't seen him gracing the pews at church either. Of course, that could be because Myrtle's attendance was a bit on the spotty side.

Surely, the man did something relaxing in his free time! Did he just go home and lie around on his sofa eating cheese dip and watching television?

Her ruminating was interrupted by a hesitant-sounding knock on her front door. Myrtle raised her eyebrows in surprise, putting aside her empty notepad. She was about to pull open the door without looking, when Red's dire warnings about lurking murderers popped into her head. Myrtle looked cautiously out the window next to her door.

Annette Dawson stood there, giving her a reassuring-I'm-not-a-killer smile. It was probably her "nurse face" that she would give patients before taking their blood or giving them a shot. Myrtle unlocked her door and opened it. "Good for you for being careful, Miss Myrtle. I can't imagine how you're able to sleep a wink at night. Two bodies in your yard!" Then she unexpectedly misted up, fishing in her purse for a tissue. Apparently, her own mention of a body had reminded her about Charles's untimely death.

Myrtle made all the appropriate concerned noises and ushered Annette to a comfy chair. "It's all still really upsetting, isn't it?"

Annette gave Myrtle a relieved smile. "It really is, Miss Myrtle. Of course, you wouldn't know that Charles and I were friends."

Myrtle tried to come up with a surprised expression but utterly failed, only conjuring a frozen look.

Annette gave a chuckle that sounded like a sob. "So the gossip got all over town, did it? You obviously know we were more than just ordinary friends."

There was really no point in denying it at this point. "That's pretty typical for Bradley, you know. When I gave birth to Red, the town knew about it before my husband even did. News travels fast here."

Annette nodded ruefully. "That's what my husband was telling me. Silas said that the entire town knew about Charles and me and that he was a laughingstock."

"I don't think he's a laughingstock. This is fairly mild in Bradley, as far as scandals go," said Myrtle in a comforting voice. Well, except for the murder part of it.

Annette suddenly got a stubborn set to her chin that Myrtle recognized from the reception when she'd argued with Silas. "There really wasn't anything dishonorable about Charles's and my relationship. That's because it was a love match. I *had* to spend time with Charles," said Annette, leaning forward and peering intently at Myrtle as if looking to see if she believed her. "That's what Silas doesn't understand."

She *bet* he didn't understand it.

"He was so mad when he found out about us. He said these horrible things to Charles," said Annette with a shudder.

"Horrible?" asked Myrtle, mind racing. "Horrible like what?"

"He said he was going to kill Charles," said Annette, looking down at her hands. "Of course he didn't mean a word of it," she added quickly. "He was shocked when he heard that Charles was dead."

"But that didn't mean that he was going to be happy about you going to the funeral," said Myrtle.

"Exactly. He flat-out told me not to go. He couldn't stop me, though. After all, I wanted to pay my respects to Charles." Annette teared up again.

Bypassing the waterworks, Myrtle said quickly, "I did notice that Silas was trying to steer you out of my house during the reception. He was still pretty angry about the whole thing."

Annette nodded. "Like I said, he was furious. It was all because he thought the whole town knew about my affair." She shrugged. "I guess they did, too, since even you know about it."

The suggestion being that Myrtle didn't get out much.

"But I know Silas couldn't have killed Charles. He couldn't kill anybody! Even as mad as he was," said Annette.

Myrtle wanted to have an opportunity to talk to Silas and determine that for herself. "Remind me again what Silas does for a living?" she asked. Maybe she could show up at his business to question him.

"He's an electrician," said Annette.

Oof. That was pretty expensive work to have done. She'd have to see if there was something she really needed looking at. Usually, the service call alone was worth more money than she could spare from her retirement pay.

Annette was studying her curiously, as if wondering how they suddenly got on the topic of Silas's work. Myrtle added, as if she were simply making conversation, "And you're a nurse, isn't that right? At the county hospital?"

"That's right. My shift recently changed, too. Now I'm working nights there." Annette rolled her eyes. "It's not my favorite shift, but I'll adjust. That's why I'm able to be here now instead of at work." She smiled at Myrtle. "I didn't actually come over for a visit, although it's been very nice."

Myrtle had forgotten to even wonder why she'd shown up at her house.

"I was wondering if you'd come across my pocketbook. I must have put it down here at the reception and then left in such a rush that I forgot it," said Annette.

There had been no pocketbook left behind—of that, Myrtle was positive. "Didn't it have your car keys and everything in it?" asked Myrtle.

"No, I'd actually stuck my keys in my dress pocket, so I had those. By the time I realized that I'd left it, I knew the police had blocked off your house to do the forensic work. Then I forgot about it again until a little while ago." Annette sighed. "I've just had a lot on my mind lately and it's made me scattered."

"It's always a relief to hear other people say that they're forgetful," said Myrtle. "I'd hate to think it was just me. But I haven't seen your purse, Annette. I'll be sure to keep an eye out for it, though. Are you sure you left it here? What does it look like?"

Annette furrowed her brow. "That's funny. Yes, it really has to be here. I know I had it with me when I left the funeral. It's just a small, brown leather bag. It's not anywhere here?"

As if Myrtle's house was voluminous enough to have many possibilities of harboring a missing purse. "Not that I've seen," said Myrtle. "But I'll do some digging around later. And I'll ask the police if they noticed it while they were here."

"Such a horrible thing that happened during the reception," said Annette, looking in the direction of Myrtle's backyard with a shudder. "Do the police think it's tied in to Charles's death somehow?"

"I think they have to," said Myrtle. "After all, it's not like the town is full of murderers. It's a lot more likely that whoever killed Charles also murdered Lee Woosley."

Annette stood up rather quickly and said, "Such a shame. Well, I've taken up enough of your time, Miss Myrtle."

Her decision to leave was so abrupt that Myrtle wondered if Annette thought that *she* somehow had something to do with the two bodies in her backyard. "Oh, one quick question, Annette. I was...well, having a conversation with someone recently about Dr. Bass. It was mentioned that he's rarely seen around town. Do you know if he has any close friends in Bradley?"

Now Annette was grinning at her, seeming to have forgotten her misgivings. "Now, Miss Myrtle, you're not thinking of sparking a relationship with Dr. Bass, are you? He certainly is good-looking, though."

Myrtle blinked at her in horror, imagining all the gossip that would fly around town if Annette Dawson started saying that she had a crush on the dentist. The poor man would probably not even schedule appointments for her anymore. "Heavens!" she said, in protest.

Annette laughed. "I know, I know—I was only kidding, Miss Myrtle. I'm sure the dentist is young enough to be...um, your son."

Grandson, technically.

"You're probably matchmaking, aren't you?" Annette gave her a mischievous, knowing smile.

That explanation would work well. Myrtle nodded encouragingly.

Annette said, "The only person I've seen him with, and I've seen him on more than one occasion with him, is this guy with real cropped, dark hair. *Not* a woman, since I know that's what you really want to know. As far as I can tell, Dr. Bass is extremely available. Although I've heard that Peggy Neighbors is trying to make sure he's *not* available." She gave Myrtle a meaningful look.

It seemed more likely that Lee Woosley was trying to make a match between the dentist and his daughter. Peggy was hung-up on Charles Clayborne, not Hugh Bass.

"Do you know where Dr. Bass lives? I was wondering if he were someone I'd run into casually—say, if I were having a walk or something."

"He lives on the lake, but across the water from you. A pretty good-sized house," said Annette. She glanced at her watch and raised her eyebrows. "Now I really do have to go. I'm going to be late for an appointment."

Myrtle sighed. She hadn't been able to figure out an innocuous way to continue asking questions about the man with dark hair before Annette walked out her door.

Chapter Thirteen

The best thing about Annette's visit was the way she'd given Myrtle an excuse to talk to Annette's husband. Myrtle hadn't fancied calling Silas up with an electrical problem for him to take a look at—that would have set her back at least a hundred dollars—-just for him to walk through her door.

Now all Myrtle had to do is to "find" Annette's missing pocketbook and deliver it to Silas, along with a few well-phrased and pointed questions.

Myrtle was about to pick up the phone and see if Miles wanted to go with her to the store to buy a cheap purse, when she hesitated. Miles had been icy on the way back from the dentist. She'd better let him sulk it all out of his system before she asked him for another favor. Miles could nurse hurt feelings much longer than a woman could.

Still, the thought of walking to Brogan's, the small, downtown department store, wasn't particularly appealing to Myrtle. The last couple of days (and accompanying wakeful nights) had tired her out more than she wanted to admit. She'd give Elaine a call. Maybe Elaine would be up for a short shopping trip, or at least up for an opportunity to take some more appallingly bad pictures for the *Bradley Bugle*.

Fifteen minutes later, Elaine's van pulled into her driveway. "I'm always ready to get out of the house," she said, as Myrtle climbed into the front seat "but you know we're likely to have more of an adventure than you planned. I have Jack with me. Of course."

Myrtle turned to look into the back of the van and saw Jack beaming at her as he clutched his well-worn Dirty Doggy doll. "He looks like an absolute angel," said Myrtle. "I don't think he's planning to take us on any types of adventures."

Jack threw Dirty Doggy at her and laughed.

Elaine sighed. "Sweet and sour. That's Jack's mood today. I know you mentioned a short trip to the store. It could possibly end up being even shorter than you'd planned. What is it that you're shopping for again?"

"A new pocketbook," said Myrtle, holding Dirty Doggy up and making him walk and trip up on the air as Jack crowed loudly in response.

"A pocketbook?" asked Elaine, shooting Myrtle a sideways look. "Don't you have that huge shelf in your bedroom closet that's filled to bursting with large, navy purses?"

"Now, now, Elaine. They're not just navy, they're black and gray and beige, too," said Myrtle. Neutrals went with everything.

Elaine was clearly planning to ask more questions about the unusual pocketbook hunting expedition, but they were already at the department store. Plus, Jack was contemplating having an enormous meltdown.

"Did you bring your camera?" asked Myrtle. "There should be gobs of opportunities to take pictures at Brogan's."

"I figured I was juggling enough today," said Elaine. "With Jack being in an unpredictable mood and all." She lifted him out of the car and put him directly into the stroller that she'd quickly unfolded.

They walked into the ancient store and traveled up the elevator to the second floor, which had women's clothes and accessories. The elevator still had an equally ancient elevator attendant who opened the door manually for them when they arrived on the second floor. Myrtle swore she remembered the same attendant when she'd been a child at the store.

Elaine started walking to the large, neutral handbag section. "This one looks like you, Myrtle," she said, holding up a likely candidate. She rummaged on the inside, pulling out some of the paper that filled the bag. "It's got lots of pockets for your peppermints. I know how much you love stashing those away."

Myrtle looked to the very back, way-off corner of the store. "Actually, I think I'm going to look at the bargain table. You know—see what's drastically reduced."

Elaine shrugged and put down the pocketbook, following behind Myrtle with the stroller.

Myrtle gave the table a critical eye. What was the cheapest pocketbook she could find? Then she could fill it with some junk from her house and it would make the perfect prop to take to Silas Dawson's house. Everything on the table was an additional sixty percent off the lowest markdown...and she saw that one was marked down to ten dollars. She picked it up. It had a cow print on it, and fuchsia flowers near the pink straps.

"This will do," muttered Myrtle. Especially for only a few dollars.

Elaine stared at the purse. "That is the most hideous pocketbook I've ever seen. All right, Myrtle, what's up? I know you're not buying something like that for yourself."

Myrtle filled her in quickly. Elaine said, "I was wondering how everything was going with the case. But why not just use one of the millions of bags you've got in your closet?"

"Silas would suspect something if I brought one of those over, and said I thought it belonged to Annette. My pocketbooks are roomy, comfortable, and perfect for me—and they wouldn't work at all for somebody like Annette. Plus," said Myrtle with a sigh, "they look like old lady purses."

"Nothing wrong with that!" said Elaine emphatically. Then she added, "What are you hoping to find out from Silas when you see him?"

"Well, it would be lovely if he just gave up and told me that he was responsible for killing two people. Somehow, though, I'm thinking that probably won't happen. I'd love to find out if he has an alibi for the murders. And I'd also like to hear him unload about Charles Clayborne—maybe give me some more insight into the guy."

"I thought that Miles was Charles Clayborne's cousin," said Elaine with a frown. "Wasn't he able to fill you in about him?"

"Not particularly," said Myrtle dryly. "He was more concerned with making sure that I knew he really had nothing to do with Charles and that he didn't approve of him. Other than that, it was all kind of vague."

"It doesn't sound like Silas Dawson exactly had a close relationship with Charles either," pointed out Elaine. Jack was starting to struggle to get out of the stroller now to wreak havoc in the store. "He was just trying to keep himself and his wife away from Charles."

"Maybe, but people must have known Charles from when he grew up in Bradley. Silas Dawson is a little older than Charles, but they probably would have been in school at the same time—maybe he was just a grade or two ahead of Charles. I want to see what I find out." She watched as Jack started determinedly trying to unlatch his seatbelt in the stroller.

"I think he's almost figured out the seatbelt," said Elaine with a sigh. "We probably will want to wrap this up pretty soon or else Jack is going to be making a big scene. Have you decided on that purse?" She gave a shudder, looking at it.

"This is definitely the one. Just based on the price point and the fact that it's definitely not an old lady pocketbook," said Myrtle.

"It's not really an *anybody* pocketbook," said Elaine as they walked to the checkout.

Back at home, Myrtle threw a few odds and ends into the pocketbook to make it more plausible. Some tissues, spare change, an old lipstick, and a sprinkling of peppermints. Then she decided, after reflection, that the peppermints might be another tip-off that it was really a purse that Myrtle had concocted. She replaced the mints with a pack of crackers.

At slightly after seven that evening, Myrtle set out to visit with Silas Dawson. Elaine had not only volunteered to drive her there, she'd practically insisted. She stayed in the car with Jack and assured Myrtle that Red hadn't gotten back from work yet, so he wouldn't wonder what Elaine and Myrtle were up to. And with the baby.

Myrtle carefully walked up the front walkway and rang the doorbell. When there wasn't any answer, she knocked on the door, in case the doorbell wasn't working.

After a couple more minutes, Silas finally appeared at the door. He raised his eyebrows when he saw Myrtle standing there. "Yes? Miss Myrtle, isn't it? Something I can help you with?" His expression said that he couldn't really envision what that might possibly be.

Myrtle took a deep breath and held up the tacky bag. "Annette told me that she thought she might have left her pocketbook at my house during the funeral reception. Is this it?"

Silas actually took a half step back as if trying to escape from the purse. "I don't really take much note of Annette's pocketbooks," he said in a growling voice, "but I'm positive that's not one of hers. Positive." He looked relieved when Myrtle put it back in the plastic grocery bag.

Then Silas frowned again. "Annette didn't tell me she'd left her purse at your house." He rubbed his face with his hands. "She wasn't even supposed to be there."

Myrtle was trying to figure out how to carefully angle for information when Silas abruptly asked her, "You knew she was having an affair with Charles Clayborne, didn't you?" His eyes narrowed as he searched her face for the truth.

Myrtle sighed. "That's true. But it's not like everyone in the town knows it. I just happened to talk to somebody who'd heard about it."

"And then that person would have told another person, then another," said Silas. He groaned. "The whole thing is just stupid. Annette loves *me*." His tone was more questioning than sure, though.

"Of course she does," said Myrtle soundly. Especially now that Charles was gone.

Silas seemed to be able to tell which way her thoughts were heading. "But hey—I didn't have anything to do with Charles's death. I didn't even really know the guy. And there were plenty of other people who didn't like Charles."

"Who?" asked Myrtle, leaning in on her cane.

"Well, Lee Woosley for one," said Silas.

"Of course, he's dead now, too," reminded Myrtle.

"Oh yeah," said Silas in a deflated voice. Then he added quickly, "But he still could have killed Charles before he died. Then somebody else killed Lee."

"Clearly," said Myrtle, holding back a sigh. Silas didn't seem like the brightest bulb in the box. Which was weird, because electricians were usually bright. No pun intended.

"Do you know why Lee hated Charles so much?" asked Myrtle. "I heard about the fight at the poker game. But it seems extreme to go hunt the man down because he cheated at poker."

"That's the kind of man Charles Clayborne was, though," said Silas bitterly. "He was a cheater. He made my wife cheat on me, he cheated at cards, and I bet he cheated at business, too. Yeah, that can make somebody mad enough to murder. But Lee had other reasons, too."

Myrtle just held her breath and waited. Silas was chatty, and she wondered if that might have something to do with the faint whiff of beer she'd detected.

Sure enough, he kept right on talking. "I remember Charles from way back. We were never friends, though, like I said. But people talked about him sometimes, and I saw him around the high school. He was a bad guy even then. He'd brag about how he cheated on tests and outsmarted the system, that kind of thing. He acted like stupid people were the ones who would follow all the rules, study, and get good grades the old-fashioned way."

Silas continued, "He also dated a whole slew of different girls. One of them was Peggy. Peggy Woosley, she was then. Peggy was a friend of my little sister, so I did know her. Real sweet girl. You could tell that she thought that Charles Clayborne hung the moon."

"And I'm guessing that Charles didn't exactly return her affections," said Myrtle. She was liking Charles less and less. No wonder Miles had practically disavowed being related to him.

"Of course not. But, regardless, she was head-over-heels with the dolt. He took advantage of that fact, too, apparently. The night before I heard about Charles's murder," said Silas, lowering his voice, "Lee was trying to make me feel better about Annette's affair with Charles. We were sitting in a bar and Lee told me that Charles had gotten Peggy pregnant their senior year of high school."

Myrtle's eyes widened. This must have been a well-kept secret for her not to have heard a thing about it.

"Charles convinced Peggy that he was going to marry her and that they were going to have this perfect little life together. But he ran away from Bradley the minute he graduated. Wonder if he had a suspicion that Peggy was going to have a baby?" Silas shook his head.

"This is such a small town that I'm shocked that nobody knew about this," said Myrtle, knitting her brows.

"Oh, they knew Peggy was pregnant, all right," said Silas with a short laugh. "But they thought it was Jim Neighbors' baby. Remember how she used to be married to him?"

Myrtle nodded slowly. "She got divorced ages ago, didn't she?"

"A couple of years after they married. The baby was just two. Jim had always had a fondness for Peggy, and Lee sweetened the pot by offering him a job doing repairs and light contracting with him," said Silas.

"I see. That would have avoided a big scandal here in Bradley, for sure," said Myrtle.

"The funny thing," said Silas, "is that Peggy never forgot Charles. She still loved him, after all that, according to her dad." He stopped and sighed. "That part actually maybe I do understand. I still love Annette, too, no matter if she has been running around on me. Apparently, Peggy tried to get back together with Charles as soon as he showed back up here in town."

The poor, confused thing. How could she not see the kind of man Charles was?

"Lee told me that he strung her along again, same as last time. Then Peggy started hearing that Charles was seeing Annette. And probably some other women, too. She was totally devastated. Peggy finally told him the truth, too—that her daughter, now almost eighteen, was his," said Silas.

Myrtle leaned forward more on her cane. Her feet, never very cooperative, were starting to actively hurt now, but she ignored it and hung on to Silas's every word.

"Miss Myrtle, you should have seen old Lee's face when he was telling me this story. It was red as all get-out. Don't know if he was more mad, or frustrated, or about to cry. Lee told me that Charles laughed when Peggy told him about his daughter. Then he scoffed about it—saying that he didn't believe her. Apparently, Peggy ran off back home and cried her eyes out," said Silas, shaking his head. "That Charles sure was some character. Red's going to have quite a time figuring out who did it. Half the town wanted Charles dead.

Myrtle closed the van door and buckled up as Elaine started driving her back home. "I take it Silas didn't claim the hideous handbag," she noted drily. Jack was talking to himself in the backseat and Myrtle turned to smile at him.

"No, he sure didn't. But he did tell me why Lee hated Charles Clayborne. It had a whole lot to do with his daughter Peggy and not much to do with cheating at poker." Myrtle filled Elaine in on the way home. "I can't imagine that Lee would have wanted Charles to get back together with his daughter—but I bet he wanted him to put some money up to support her college tuition or other care."

"Wow," said Elaine finally. "And people think that nothing happens in small towns."

"The whole parade of human drama happens in small towns," said Myrtle. "It just happens on a small scale, that's all."

"So what I'm getting from this tale of woe," said Elaine slowly, "is that Peggy definitely had a motive to kill Charles. She'd put her heart and soul into loving him and she was coldly and cruelly rejected; not once, but twice."

"Revenge is surely a powerful motivator," said Myrtle. "Don't forget about her father, either. Lee Woosley was plenty mad at Charles Clayborne. How much can a father really take before he starts taking it out on the guy who's at the bottom of the mess?"

"But if he killed Charles, then who killed Lee?"

"What if Peggy did it out of anger? What if, no matter how irrationally, she was still crazy about Charles? She might have struck out against her father for killing the man she loved so much," said Myrtle.

Elaine sighed. "I guess so. It just seems very far-fetched to me."

"I'm amazed at just how often life resembles my soap opera. *Tomorrow's Promise* really hits the nail on the head sometimes. It's more like watching a documentary than a daytime drama."

"Uh-oh," said Elaine as they pulled up to Myrtle's driveway. "Looks like you've got some company."

Chapter Fourteen

Myrtle noticed with horror that Erma Sherman was standing on her front step. Erma grinned and waved as the van drove up the drive.

"Now how am I going to escape that?" moaned Myrtle. "Why can't the woman remember that she lives *next door* and that she needs to stay over there? All she does is pester me."

"Just tell her you've had a big day shopping with me and Jack and you need to go in and put your feet up and close your eyes for a while," said Elaine in a sympathetic voice. "She should understand that."

But it took a lot for Myrtle to admit to someone, even falsely, that she was tired out. She liked to present a picture to the world of strength and heartiness. "Of all the neighbors in the world, I had to get *her*."

"She's my neighbor too," said Elaine. She chuckled. "For some reason Red and I aren't on Erma's radar at all. She'd prefer to bother you."

"That's because she doesn't like children. Or animals," said Myrtle, glancing around. Where was that Pasha when she needed her? The cat was the one protection she had against that woman.

"I thought she was always feeding the birds and stuff like that."

"The squirrels. Erma Sherman feeds the squirrels. And that right there should show how squirrelly *she* is," said Myrtle. She reluctantly opened the car door and stepped outside. "Wish me luck."

There was just no point avoiding the inevitable. Erma Sherman was bound and determined to have some kind of visit with her, and by golly, that's what she was going to get. If Myrtle caved in, then maybe Erma would leave her alone for a while. Besides, standing at the ill-mannered Silas's door for such a long time (hadn't the man realized she was *old*?) meant that she was ready to sit for a while with her feet up—even if it meant she had to suffer through a chat with Erma. Maybe she should pull that burned-up ham out of the fridge and offer Erma a sandwich. That might scare her off from visiting for a while.

As she walked down the front walk, Erma said in a hurry, "I know you've got to run Myrtle, but I needed to tell you something. You're always in such a rush! Don't you think you're going to fall down and break a hip or something? Moving slower is better."

Myrtle resisted the urge to shoot her a sour look for the unasked-for advice. But she was being good, no matter how torturous it was. She hoped she was winning a few points for this from the big guy upstairs.

Erma's mouth dropped open in complete shock as Myrtle fished her keys out from her pocketbook, opened the door and motioned her inside. "It's such a warm day today, Erma. Why don't you come inside and tell me what's on your mind."

Erma trotted in before Myrtle could change her mind. As Myrtle closed the front door behind her, she glimpsed Elaine across the street, looking her way in shock. Elaine would likely be checking back in with her later to make sure she hadn't suffered a small stroke.

Once Myrtle sat down, she had a feeling that she wasn't going to be getting back up again for a while. "Erma, just hold that thought and give me a few minutes to get settled." She definitely wanted to make a quick visit to the bathroom—she'd been gone for a long while, after all—then pour them both some iced tea and get them out a small snack. Erma, from what she remembered, could be a fairly demanding visitor and it would irritate the stew out of Myrtle to keep having to jump up from her chair like a jumping jack.

She returned a few minutes later with a tray holding a plastic pitcher of sweet tea, two tall glasses, and a plate with cheese and crackers on it. Myrtle noticed wryly that Erma didn't leap up to help her carry in the tray, despite the fact that Myrtle was holding the tray with one arm and her cane with the other. Typical Erma.

But, since she was determined to make this visit stick and count as a *real visit*, she hid her irritation. At least, she attempted to.

Erma was already blabbing on about some horrible medical problem she was having with her skin that was making Myrtle lose whatever appetite she had. Myrtle decided that she was going to have to interrupt Erma, or else terminate the visit. She was about to cut her off with a quick retort, but bit her lip and took in a deep breath.

Myrtle mildly said, "Erma, hate to interrupt you, but before I forget—you know how memory is with older adults—I think you mentioned you wanted to tell me something? I thought it might be something about the case."

Clearly, though, there was a reason why she'd never used this kinder, gentler tack with Erma in the years she'd known her. That's because, Erma bulldozed over 'kind and gentle' like they didn't even exist.

"So that was my day at the dermatologist," she said. "But it wasn't over then! Next, I had to go to the dentist. Can you believe it? The dentist!" Erma grinned at her and Myrtle decided that she could certainly believe it. Erma's teeth were not in the best of shape. And Erma's breath had an unfortunate hint of gingivitis about it.

The dentist! And Erma's favorite activity besides hunting down and torturing Myrtle, was flirting with men. No matter how hopeless that flirting might be. She must, absolutely *must*, be one of Dr. Bass's patients.

"Do you go to Dr. Bass?" asked Myrtle quickly, while Erma was taking in a quick breath.

She beamed. "I do! I do go to Dr. Bass. And he and I are very good friends, too," Erma said proudly.

This sounded very much like one of Erma's chronic delusions. Myrtle very much hoped that just a fraction of that statement was true, and that maybe Erma could at least tell her who Dr. Bass's friends actually *were*.

"So you see Dr. Bass outside of the dental office?" asked Myrtle.

Erma was reluctant to answer this. Finally, she said, "Well, we would, except that Dr. Bass's business takes up so much of his time. Especially since he's the only dentist in town. But I've mentioned to him before that I would love to go to the movies, or out to eat with him whenever he had a break in his busy schedule."

Myrtle was sure the dentist took that under advisement and stayed as busy as he possibly could.

"He has this huge house on the lake," said Erma, her eyes lighting up. "It's right on the opposite side of the lake from us. And he has a couple of boats—a bigger one and a little one. I've seen him out on them when I've been out boating."

If you could *call* what Erma did *boating*. She had an ancient pontoon boat.

"But of course we see a lot of each other because of my dental visits. I have a lot of dental visits because of these problems I keep having with my teeth," said Erma.

Before Erma could spin off into another revolting health-related discussion, Myrtle quickly broke in.

"You know, I was talking with someone the other day about Dr. Bass. I don't think I've really ever noticed the man hanging out around Bradley. Oh, I might have seen him getting food at the grocery store or something, but that's about it. But someone mentioned that he had a friend—a male friend," said Myrtle quickly, since Erma would have denied that Dr. Bass had any female friends other than herself. "Do you know who that might be?"

Erma puffed up with pride. This time Myrtle thought that maybe she did actually know something.

"That would have to be Dr. Bass's friend from high school." Erma leaned in so much to tell gossip that she looked like she might break in half. "He's a very handsome man—a barber. You probably know him."

"Except that I don't go to barbers for haircuts," said Myrtle pointedly.

"You must have noticed him around town, anyway. He's a fine dresser—wears pink ties to his barbershop and always a lot of cologne. I love seeing him when I'm out at the store or post office or something. He smells delicious and he always winks at me!" Erma giggled. If Myrtle was to believe Erma, then she had a beau in every port.

"So they're still friends then," said Myrtle. "I wonder if Dr. Bass confides much in this fellow. What's his name?"

"Buddy Fenton. His shop isn't on the square in downtown—it's farther out," said Erma.

"Very interesting," said Myrtle. She hesitated. Erma had wanted to see her to tell her something. Although it was something that Myrtle probably didn't care about hearing, if she didn't tell Myrtle, then she was going to continue trying to talk to her until she did. Myrtle sighed. "Erma, wasn't there something you wanted to tell me about?"

Erma squinted up her rodent-like features and studied Myrtle's ceiling in thought. "Yes, there was. Let's see. It wasn't about my dermatology appointment, although I talked about that. It wasn't about my dentist appointment, although we talked about that, too." She winked at Myrtle, giving her the horrible impression that she was going to spread news of Myrtle's fascination with Dr. Bass all over town.

"Let's see. It had something to do with the murder I'm sure. And I wanted to tell you because you always snoop around for the paper. Think, Erma! Think!" Erma put her hands on both sides of her head and pushed, as if she could squeeze the memory out of her brain.

Erma snapped her fingers. "I've got it! It was the morning that Lee was murdered in your yard. Before we all went to the funeral. I had the feeling that someone was watching our houses from the bushes near the lake. Of course, it was probably Miles, since he must have killed Charles."

Both Erma and Myrtle's yards sloped down from a level, grassy yard (or weedy yard, if you were talking about Erma's) through a wooded area down to the lake. Myrtle had an old dock down there and a boat. It wasn't actually her boat anymore—she'd not wanted the bother of upkeep anymore and had handed the keys over to Red.

Myrtle waited for Erma to say something more newsworthy—that she had seen a man dressed all in black, or that she'd noticed footprints behind the azalea bushes near the lake—something meatier than a funny feeling. But this was all Erma apparently had.

Myrtle cleared her throat. "Duly noted. Thanks, Erma."

Yes, Erma had been unexpectedly helpful. Who'd have thought? But of course, she was still going to need to formulate a plan so that Erma didn't keep visiting with her. This visit, for instance, had been entirely too pleasant. Erma would likely be eager to repeat it.

"You know," said Myrtle in a confiding voice. "I'm glad you came over today. There's been a couple of different things that I wanted to share with you."

"Really?" Erma looked surprised and just a wee bit uncomfortable. It was the discomfort factor that Myrtle was going after.

"Yes. One thing I wanted to do was show you some of my old photo albums. Now that Elaine has this interest in photography, it's made me even more interested in taking a look at some of my own pictures. I think I had quite an eye for composition, and I'm considering taking it back up!" Myrtle gestured to a row of ancient photo albums on the bookcase across the room. "Would you take five or six of those albums out for me? This shouldn't take too long—maybe a couple of hours. You have the time to spend with me, don't you?"

Erma was definitely looking alarmed now. "No, not really. Not right now, Myrtle."

"Oh, you have some place to go? How about tomorrow? Maybe tomorrow afternoon?"

"I'm pretty sure I have another doctor's appointment tomorrow, Myrtle. Sorry." Erma stood up and hastily walked toward Myrtle's kitchen, carrying her dirty glass to put in the sink.

"Well then, the next day, surely. You won't believe these pictures, Erma. There are some of the cutest pictures of Red you've ever seen. You'll just love them," said Myrtle.

Erma used a very firm, un-Erma-like voice. "I'm going to have to call you later and let you know when I've got time to sit with you and look through albums. It might take a while, though—I've been very, very busy lately!"

Now Erma was hurrying to the door. "See you soon, Myrtle. Or, well, if not soon, then some time."

That was the quickest she'd ever dispatched Erma Sherman. The quickest, at least, when Pasha hadn't been involved in the process.

Thinking about Pasha made Myrtle miss the cat, who hadn't been around the house that day. This made her get angry with herself for missing a feral cat. She was sure the cat didn't miss *her*. She wondered if Pasha was still miffed by the fact that Myrtle had held her against her will in her bedroom during the reception.

Myrtle's thinking about the reception reminded her about the ham again. She bet the cat really would love some of it. And it still annoyed her that she'd spent so much money on a ham and hadn't been able to use it. Maybe she'd just freeze the ham. Then she could cut off bits of it later on for a soup...and give a few bites to Pasha, too. Right now, with the case and everything, she just didn't have time to deal with it, but later she would. She took the ham out of the fridge and put it in the freezer.

That night, Myrtle was visited by her usual insomnia. She might even have had the faintest hint of uneasiness. She looked out her kitchen window into the backyard—with a small degree of apprehension.

It was hard to tell in the dark, and with the grass as tall as it was, but it looked as if something was out there in her yard. The hairs on the back of Myrtle's neck started rising. No, there was definitely something out there in that same space among the gnomes.

Myrtle held her breath as she fumbled with the light switch beside the door, accidentally turning on both the kitchen light and the grinding garbage disposal, cursing at herself as she did. She finally got the right one and peered anxiously out into the suddenly illuminated yard.

Pasha the cat lay in the spot where the bodies had been. She blinked at Myrtle in the light but showed no inclination to get up. She was glad to see the cat but didn't want to disturb her from...whatever it was that Pasha was doing out there.

Did the spot smell odd to Pasha? Was there suddenly good nighttime hunting in Myrtle's backyard? Or was Pasha, as Myrtle strongly suspected, standing guard?

"Myrtle, I already have a barber," said Miles coldly.

"Sometimes it's nice, though, to shake things up a little bit, Miles. You know—to get a different perspective on your hairstyle from another professional," said Myrtle.

Miles's voice, coming through the phone, sounded quite icy. "I don't have a *hairstyle*. My hair is just a standard men's style. And I just got my hair cut two weeks ago...I don't need a haircut."

"It seemed to me that your hair was coming down kind of low over your ears," said Myrtle judiciously. "You could go to have it shaped up a bit."

There was a meaningful silence on the other end of the line.

"Oh, come on, Miles. What's the harm in it? I'll even pay for the haircut. If you hate the way this fellow cuts your hair, then it's going to grow back in a few weeks anyway. I can't think of another way to talk to Buddy Fenton without visiting his house as a reporter for the paper—and I have a feeling he won't dish on his old friend Dr. Bass if I'm representing the paper. What do you say?"

"I say that I think my own barber will get mad at me if I see a different barber. Then I'll really be in a mess," said Miles. His mind was clearly working overtime.

"Pooh on that! Barbers aren't like beauticians—they're not going to be hypersensitive and get their feelings hurt just because you try someplace different," said Myrtle.

There was a heavy sigh on the other end of the phone. "All right, I give up. But this better not end up getting me in trouble with my barber, Myrtle."

"It won't," said Myrtle with satisfaction. "And at least this visit won't result in some discovered cavities."

Miles took an instant dislike to the barber as they waited for him to finish up with the client he had in the chair.

"He must have bathed in cologne," said Miles, wrinkling up his nose.

"He's a single guy. He's just trying to make sure he's attractive to the ladies."

"In a barbershop? What ladies is he going to see in here?" asked Miles.

"Well, I'm in here."

Miles raised his eyebrows. "Yes, and you're the only one. Besides, how are we going to explain your presence in here? Are you my mother?"

"Very funny. I'm not old enough to be your mother, as you well know." Actually, that wasn't entirely true, so she kept breezily talking, "We'll tell the barber that you're not really driving anymore and rely on me for rides."

Miles gave her a baleful look.

"He's not going to ask anyway. Why would he care that I'm here or what my relationship to you is?" asked Myrtle.

Apparently, however, that was just what Buddy Fenton was interested in. He immediately remarked that Myrtle was the first woman he'd seen in the shop for the last couple of weeks. "Are you just coming along to make sure he gets enough taken off?" Buddy asked Myrtle, with a wink at Miles.

"Oh, Myrtle?" asked Miles, in an offhanded voice that meant trouble. "She's my designated driver. I always have a few cocktails with my lunch. Myrtle drives me around town afterward." He sounded convincingly slurred.

Buddy gave a hearty laugh, slapping Miles on the back as if they were in some kind of men's club together.

"I like the way you've set up your day," said Buddy, putting a cape around Miles. "That's the life, isn't it? I guess one day, after I'm retired, I'll be able to do the same thing. You only have time for hedonism when you're real young or real old, right?"

Miles had a wistful expression on his face, which made Myrtle smile. She knew that he hadn't experienced hedonism during either young or old.

Myrtle cleared her throat. "So you did have a wild youth then, Buddy? Who all did you go to high school with? I'd already retired when you came through Bradley High, hadn't I?"

"You sure had, Mrs. Clover. And that's just as well for you—you wouldn't have wanted to deal with my crowd, I bet. I was in there with Charles Clayborne and Hugh Bass—hung out with them."

Myrtle said innocently. "Oh! That sounds like a wild crowd, for sure. I was so sorry about Charles. What a tragedy."

Buddy carefully trimmed a spot above Miles's ear. "It was, wasn't it? Of course, it wasn't like I'd kept in touch with Charles. Nobody had from our group. Well, except for Hugh." He suddenly stopped talking and pressed his lips together as if he hadn't planned on saying that.

"Charles left Bradley soon after he graduated, didn't he?" asked Myrtle. "So how did Dr. Bass keep up with him? Just online and by phone?"

Buddy said slowly, "Not just that way, no. Hugh Bass ended up at the same college that Charles did. Of course, Charles wasn't planning on being a dentist." Buddy smirked at the thought of Charles going into dentistry.

"What was Charles thinking of going into?" asked Miles. He quickly hiccupped, in case his question had sounded too sober. Myrtle noticed that he didn't claim any kinship to Charles.

"Anything shady," said Buddy smoothly. "Charles wasn't exactly a guy who minded operating on both sides of the law." He stepped back to give his work a critical eye, then continued. "I'm not saying that Charles did anything outright illegal...in an *obvious* way, anyway. He wasn't out there robbing banks, dealing drugs or breaking into cars or houses. But if there was something in the gray area that might make him some money, or some way to hustle some money on a phony business deal? Charles was going to be up for it."

Myrtle said, frowning, "Then why did Dr. Bass stay friends with him?"

Buddy Fenton tilted his head to the side and studied her. Summing her up probably, to see if she was just a harmless, nosy old lady. Then he glanced over at Miles. Miles hiccupped in a comforting way again and Buddy continued, "At first, I guess he thought that Charles was fun to be around. He was, you know. As long as he wasn't trying to squeeze money out of you somehow, he could be the life of the party. He could tell jokes that would leave you rolling on the floor. And he had lots of exciting ideas for things to do, too."

"But after that?" asked Myrtle. "After Dr. Bass maybe got tired of his shenanigans?"

Both Myrtle and Miles hung on Buddy's words. For a guy like Buddy, this must have been very flattering. Myrtle could tell he was the kind of person who thrived in the spotlight and craved it. He wore attention-getting cologne and had the whole look-at-me attitude that she remembered so well from students when she taught school.

But he was also Hugh Bass's friend. From all appearances, he was Hugh Bass's *only* friend. It might take a little persuading for him to disclose whatever dirt he had on Hugh and Charles, despite how much he longed to have a captive audience.

Myrtle quickly lied, "You know, I'm friends with Dr. Bass's parents. Sweet people."

Buddy smiled and combed Miles's hair, taking small snips with his scissors. "Yes, they are."

"They told me a story a couple of years back which I just barely remember. It was something to do with Dr. Bass and some trouble he'd gotten into while he'd still lived out of town." Myrtle gave a ferociously thoughtful frown, as if the fascinating story was right there on the very edge of her subconscious and just waiting for her to spill it. She tapped her nose with a long finger as if that would help her to remember it.

Buddy looked sharply at her. He glanced around the shop to ensure they were truly alone. "So you know about what happened then. I'm surprised—I didn't think that anybody knew that story. The only reason I know about it is because I was still good friends with him at the time. We're friends now, of course, but we were a lot closer back then. I've been real careful not to say anything about it."

"I know the story, yes. Dr. Bass's folks were so worried at the time. Distraught. Anyone would be! I used to know all the details, but now I've forgotten," stressed Myrtle, trying to appear foggy, vague, and hesitant.

Miles gave a few encouraging hiccups.

"Yes, so they went to a college in West Virginia. After graduation, Charles found some sort of work nearby and Hugh Bass went to dental school. This arrangement lasted for about four years. They were even roommates, trying to cut costs and share expenses. They still hung out together after Charles was done with work and when Hugh was out of class for the day. Hugh graduated and set up a practice, but they needed money. Whatever Charles was doing wasn't bringing in a whole lot, and Hugh didn't have any money to speak of, because he was paying back his tuition and paying rent for his new dental practice."

"What did they do?" asked Myrtle. "I mean," she added quickly, "remind me again what they did."

Chapter Fifteen

"Charles persuaded Hugh he should do some funny business with the billing," said Buddy, studying Myrtle carefully as if assessing how much she really knew about the whole business.

Myrtle nodded. "That's right," she said. She hesitated, trying to think how this might have been done. "So Dr. Bass started billing insurance companies for work he hadn't actually done on the patients?" It was a wild guess.

But it was an accurate one. Buddy nodded again. "Yep. Billing for fillings and crowns when he'd only done a cleaning. That kind of thing. Of course it caught up to him eventually."

Miles shot her a look. She had a feeling that he wasn't going to soon forgive her for forcing him to get his teeth looked at by a criminal.

"Jail time," she hazarded.

"Exactly. He owned up to everything and had a clean record up to that time, so he got off with the bare minimum," said Buddy.

"But his dental license would have been revoked in West Virginia, of course," murmured Myrtle in sudden, horrified realization.

Buddy gave her a quick sideways glance and shrugged. He appeared to be searching for something to say, probably on a completely different and distracting topic.

Miles continued glaring at Myrtle, momentarily forgetting his hiccups.

Myrtle said, still following the previous train of thought, "So when Charles came back into town, was he here to make trouble? Could he have been trying to blackmail Dr. Bass? Have you any idea what he was doing in town, Buddy?"

"I'm not a hundred percent positive," drawled Buddy, "but my general impression of Charles is that, if he was heading your way to talk to you, you probably ought to quickly cross to the other side of the street. I haven't known him not to try and stir up trouble. I know he never visited Hugh while he was serving time and split out of West Virginia just as fast as he could. He didn't own up to the fact that he'd been the one to hatch the fraud to begin with. He was just an all-around bad egg."

Miles was very quiet as he drove away from the barbershop. He'd insisted on driving his own car, even if it meant blowing his cover. Myrtle's teacher radar had gone off as he followed her to his car—she was sure he was making faces at her back.

Miles courteously, or out of habit, pulled up into her driveway instead of making her walk from his. Reviewing the case would be better than this silence. She did want to get Miles's opinion on some of the things that had happened. But it seemed as if he were waiting for her to get out of the car.

Myrtle cleared her throat. "I thought that was a very interesting field trip, Miles. Buddy sure made a case for Hugh Bass having a motive, whether he thought he was doing that or not."

Miles didn't respond, so she hurried on. "I still like Silas Dawson for the murderer, too. After all, crimes of passion happen all the time and he sure is wild about Annette. Then we have Peggy Neighbors, who is another crime of passion example. She must have been devastated when her advances to Charles were rejected; it must have reminded her of when she was back in high school and he left town without ever looking back."

Miles made a grumbly sound that Myrtle could distinguish as agreement or disagreement.

She kept talking. "Peggy's father, according to Silas, was very upset with Charles for hurting his daughter again. Lee could have killed Charles and then someone else took revenge on Lee for the murder. Maybe even Peggy!"

This time there was a definite eye-roll from Miles. And now, Myrtle was ready to get any kind of a reaction from him. "So that's our suspect roundup right now. Dr. Bass, Silas Dawson, Peggy Neighbors, and Lee Woosley. Or...and you, of course."

"Or you!" Miles jumped in. "You're the one with all the bodies in your yard, Myrtle. Maybe you killed these men because you were bored and wanted something to do."

Myrtle was about to give him a blistering retort, but decided it might be better for him to air whatever his grievances were and get them out of his system.

Miles's expression was morose as he looked in the mirror. Was he more depressed about hearing more dirt about his cousin or about his haircut? It did seem shorter than it usually did.

"Hair grows back, Miles," said Myrtle, starting to feel irritated. The ride back had been a fairly whiny one. She was sure that her darling grandson never sounded quite as annoying as Miles had on this car ride.

"I know that. But for the next few weeks, I'm going to be subjected to looking at this super-short hair in my bathroom mirror."

Myrtle blinked at him. He was more irritated than usual as he gripped the steering wheel. "It looks good to me, Miles. It's short, but it's not a bad haircut."

"And that guy's cologne gave me a headache," grumbled Miles. "I think he must have bathed in the stuff."

"I've got ibuprofen in my pocketbook," said Myrtle, digging around in the huge gray handbag.

"Plus I've got a follow-up visit to have a cavity filled by a convicted felon."

Myrtle said slowly, "Is what he did a felony, though? Or just run-of-the-mill illegal activity? Or possibly even just a case of regrettable judgment?"

"The fellow could be a killer, Myrtle! It's starting to look like my cousin Charles came to town specifically to blackmail Hugh Bass for opening up a practice while having a revoked license."

"I'm sure his license was only revoked in West Virginia. It's more likely that Charles was trying to blackmail Dr. Bass over the jail time. And I bet that wasn't the *only* reason he came to town. He probably also tried to scam a few people while he was here," Myrtle said with a shrug.

"Regardless. The point is that you put my teeth in the hands of a criminal who might be a murderer!"

"It was nice of me to host a reception for you," reminded Myrtle in a small voice. She thought that she might have brought this point up before, but found the event worthy of a repeat mention.

"During which the body of a local resident appeared in your backyard."

"Although that had nothing to do with me," said Myrtle. It was, however, a point that she wasn't altogether sure of.

"One *might* make the argument," said Miles, "that being friends with you is bad for my health."

"Might they?" asked Myrtle. She sighed. She did tend to have blinders on when she was investigating a mystery. She did feel that Miles was taking it all a little too far, though.

"I think," said Miles distantly, "that it would be good for my sanity, my blood pressure, and my general health if you and I took a short break from each other. Perhaps just during the course of this case."

"A trial separation?" asked Myrtle. Unfortunately, the mental image of her and Miles engaged in troubled matrimony made her give a gasping laugh and Miles's expression told her he didn't really appreciate that.

"I'm glad that you're taking this so seriously," said Miles coldly.

Myrtle looked sadly at him. His feelings were truly hurt this time. "Miles...." She said quickly, holding out a hand to him.

He kept staring determinedly straight ahead at her house. Miles could be just as stubborn as she was. Funny how she hadn't noticed that before. She sighed.

"I'll keep out of your hair for a while then," she said. Miles cringed a bit at the mention of hair. Myrtle climbed out of the car, fumbling with the car door and her cane. "Thanks for going with me today," she said before she shut the door.

What was she going to do without her sidekick? And, truth be told, her chauffer. It had been a discouraging day so far.

Myrtle walked into her house and noticed that her back door was unlocked and very slightly ajar. Had she been so absent-minded this morning that she didn't even secure the door when she left food out for Pasha? She slowly walked through her house, looking around her carefully and listening out for any sounds to indicate an intruder was inside.

Nothing seemed broken, stolen or damaged. She still had her TV, which is probably the only thing a thief would be interested in. This was a relief, because she was hoping to numb her mind by watching soap operas. Myrtle continued scanning the room and frowned. Had she left her notebooks on the kitchen table? She remembered leaving them next to the computer on her desk in the living room. And the candy bowl full of peppermints—had she really wandered off with it and stuck it on top of her fireplace mantle?

This evidence of her declining mental aptitude discouraged her even further. She made a point of double-checking that she'd locked both her back and front doors, and spent the remainder of her afternoon in an orgy of self-pity in front of her tapes of *Tomorrow's Promise* and a large bowl of chocolate ice cream. With chocolate syrup on top.

Myrtle had expected that the unsettling argument with Miles would result in a sleepless night. Sure enough, although she'd fallen asleep at the very early hour of nine o'clock, she was wide-awake at one.

She stared at the ceiling for a few minutes instead of getting up, trying to rediscover that elusive thread of sleep.

Instead of getting sleepier, her mind grew even more active. She found herself fretting over Miles and regretting the part she'd played in making him so angry and frustrated. That certainly didn't help her get any sleepier.

Unfortunately, that led to thoughts about the case and a sudden feeling of insecurity. What was she thinking? Here she was, an octogenarian woman of apparently uncertain memory, trying to conduct a murder investigation. How was she possibly going to be able to do that? There was a completely able-bodied police department here in town, led by her completely able-bodied son. They were even assisted by the state police, who all were terrifyingly efficient. Really, what was the use? She should just stay at home and figure out how to knit something and burn cookies and stay safe.

Myrtle frowned. Was that a noise in her backyard? It seemed as if it was coming from that direction. She quickly got up out of bed, put her robe on, and grabbed her cane from the side of the bed. She stuck a flashlight into her robe pocket. And, because she detested those books and movies where the heroine stupidly meandered into dark, dangerous locations after killers, she picked up a butcher knife on her way through the kitchen.

She looked through the window into her yard. There was definitely a shadowy figure out there among the tall grass gnomes—too tall to be a gnome. Too active to be a garden gnome, too. She changed her cane to her other hand, grasped the butcher knife in her right hand, and then frowned again. How was she supposed to open the stupid door while holding a cane and a knife? It was all very aggravating to be a superhero at this age. She chose the knife over the cane, yanked the door open, gave a yodeling battle cry, and charged at the figure with the knife raised.

The figure gave a braying scream of terror. "Stop! Myrtle! Help!"

Myrtle lowered the knife with one hand and fished out the flashlight, awkwardly, with her left hand. She turned it on and trained it on the alarmed face of Erma Sherman. Erma had fortunately dropped her own weapon—a baseball bat—on the ground.

"Erma!" she bellowed. "What are you doing out here?"

Myrtle looked around her and saw there were broken eggs all over her gnomes. "What have you done?" Erma Sherman as a killer? Annoying, yes. The worst neighbor ever, yes. Someone who purposefully fed squirrels and allowed crabgrass and chickweed to flourish in her yard and creep over into Myrtle's? Yes. But a murderer—she just couldn't see it.

Erma said, "Nothing! I haven't done anything, Myrtle. But somebody came out in your yard and threw eggs at your gnomes. Somebody's trying to rattle you." Erma pointed at a light shining garishly from her patio next door. "I got tired of having dead bodies turn up in the yard next to mine, so I put in a motion detector light yesterday. It cut on a few minutes ago, so I came outside to see what was going on. I guess somebody cut through my backyard to get to yours and throw some eggs."

This news didn't do much to improve Myrtle's mood. So Erma had come up with a good idea for being alerted when there was suspicious activity behind their houses. And Myrtle had, once again, not been aware of anything happening in her own backyard.

"I'm going to call Red," said Erma. "He needs to hear about this."

Myrtle grabbed Erma's sleeve. "No! Erma, Red will really shut me down if he hears about this. There's no dead body this time, just a practical joke. A mean-spirited one, but nothing deadly or dangerous."

Erma didn't look so sure. "Myrtle, somebody is setting you up as a target. A victim. Don't you think your son should know about this so he can help protect you?"

This well-meaning statement had a more irritating effect on Myrtle than all of the previous statements that Erma had ever made to her. And there had been many of them.

"I'm not a victim," said Myrtle, sounding sulky and unreasonable to her own ears.

There was a noise behind them and both women turned with a gasp, spotlighted in the beam of a strong flashlight.

It was Miles, in a navy bathrobe and slippers. He stared in silence at the odd tableau in front of him. Erma gaped at him, a baseball bat at her feet. Myrtle grasped a flashlight and a butcher knife. Egg-covered gnomes surrounded them.

"Everyone is okay," he said in a tone that was more statement than question. His gaze again flickered over the scene. "Good night," he said gruffly, and abruptly turned and left.

Erma kept nattering on about motion detectors and personal safety devices and how Red might have other ideas. Myrtle finally shut down the entire conversation by sweetly inviting Erma to come in for some milk, cookies, and a trip down memory lane with Myrtle's photo albums. Erma declined.

As Myrtle walked back in the house, she smiled to herself at the glint of interest in Miles's eyes. He was a real investigator, too, despite his insistence that he was merely a bystander. He wasn't going to be able to keep away from this case, or Myrtle, for very long. This time when Myrtle finally crawled back into bed, she fell quickly into a sound sleep.

Erma was right, decided Myrtle the next morning as she sprayed her gnomes with a garden hose. Much as she hated to admit that Erma could *ever* be right. Myrtle needed to buy something to protect herself. Getting a handgun at this point in her life wasn't a very appealing option—plus, it was Red who taught the conceal-and-carry class, and somehow she thought he wouldn't be very pleased to have his mother enroll.

Pepper spray sounded about right. If someone mucked around in her yard or her house again, she would chase them out with red pepper spray and her cane.

She had no doubt, either, that someone had come into her house. She woke up that morning with the conviction that she had *not* been imagining things, and she hadn't been losing her memory. Somebody came in her house and rearranged her stuff—probably to mess with her head.

And that person had a key. She wasn't sure how, but it was true. There had been no forced entry to her house, no broken windows, and no picked locks. No, this person had used a key.

She thought back to her middle-of-the night anxiety. She'd thought that maybe she needed to give up on investigating and play it safe. Myrtle's eyes narrowed. She was in her eighties. Wasn't the time for safety over? Who *cares* about being safe when you're an octogenarian? You've already lived a long life—no one was going to go to your funeral and exclaim what a shame it was that you'd died so young. No, what Myrtle wanted was excitement and stimulation. If she was losing her memory (and now she felt pretty sure that someone had actually been in her house and was just trying to make her feel that she was losing her memory), then she should be exercising her memory *more*. Giving it a workout. She wasn't going to just roll over. She was going to figure out who was targeting her and make them pay.

Chapter Sixteen

Myrtle walked into downtown Bradley as soon as the shops opened. There was a small sporting goods store that had been in the same location for the past sixty years. It had probably been forty years since she'd last been in there—getting a football or a baseball for Red.

This time was slightly different. The clerk looked doubtfully at her. "Red pepper spray?" he asked. "Is that something you think you'll really need here in Bradley? With a cop living right across the street from you?"

This was another former student of hers. He was elderly too, as many of her former students now were. "Look, Mike, you know what happened in my backyard; not once, but twice. I think I need all the self-protection I can get."

She'd leveled the same look at him that she had when he'd been talking in her class so many years before.

He sighed. "I won't argue with you, Mrs. Clover. I just didn't want to take advantage of you by taking your money for a product you probably won't be using, that's all."

Wasn't he *still* arguing with her, in a backhanded way? She kept staring ferociously at him as he rung up her purchase.

Once that errand was finally successfully finished, Myrtle headed home. She'd like some motion detector lights and to have her locks changed, too. Since her handyman was murdered, this was going to be tricky. She certainly didn't want to ask Red to do it, because it would start worrying him again and all she needed was to be sent to Greener Pastures retirement home.

"Dan could do it for you," said a gravelly voice behind her. Myrtle jumped violently and swung around, holding her cane out in front of her.

Wanda stood there, straggly-looking as usual, watching her with those dark eyes.

It was very disconcerting that Wanda appeared to know about the security measures that she wanted to have done at her house. "What do you mean?" asked Myrtle in a voice that came out haughtier than she'd intended.

Wanda stretched out a nicotine-stained hand to gesture at the paper bag that Myrtle carried. "You're wanting to change your locks and put up more lights, right? Same type thing as the spray. You want to be safe. Dan can help you."

Clearly, Wanda had observed her in the sporting goods store as she purchased the pepper spray. She'd probably also run into Erma this morning. No doubt, Erma was telling half the town about *her* new motion detector lights and how they helped to chase away a villain in her elderly neighbor's yard. But changing the locks? She couldn't think of a way that Wanda would know about that. Myrtle shivered. Then she shook it off.

"Crazy Dan can help me put new locks in and motion detectors?" Myrtle wasn't even sure that Dan and Wanda's hubcap-covered shack had a lock on it at all. It certainly didn't have motion detectors. It might not even consistently have electricity, depending on how often they paid their bills.

"Used to be a locksmith a long time ago," said Wanda with a shrug of an emaciated shoulder. "Sometimes does odd jobs."

"Okay," said Myrtle. "I guess he's hired, then. Can you get him to come over later this afternoon to do the jobs?"

Wanda gave her a steady look. "Since I sorta knew this was going to happen, I brought him along." She pointed across the street and Crazy Dan gave them a lackadaisical wave from where he stood, propped up against a streetlamp.

This precognition was an irritating thing. It made you feel like you were always one-step behind. "All right then," said Myrtle a bit huffily, "have your brother run by the hardware store and pick up the locks and the motion detector lights."

"Already dunnit," said Wanda. She nodded at Crazy Dan and he held up a plastic bag.

"Then have him go back to the hardware store and get a couple of extra sets of the keys," said Myrtle, through gritted teeth.

"Already dunnit," said Wanda, nodding at Crazy Dan again. Dan held up a smaller, brown bag that apparently held extra keys.

"Fine," said Myrtle. "Then I'll just meet you back at the house." Sometimes living in this town made her feel like part of a circus.

Wanda started loping off and Myrtle stopped her. "Say, Wanda, can't you tell me anything *useful*? I don't really need to know that you were five steps ahead of me on my home security project, but I'd love to know who the person behind all this is."

Wanda just looked sad. "It don't work that way."

"Don't it?" asked Myrtle. Then she sighed. She hoped Wanda and Crazy Dan's grammar wasn't catching.

"Nope. I just take the visions as they come. I been blocked on these murders," said Wanda.

"You didn't seem all that blocked the day I came to see you," said Myrtle, raising her eyebrows. "I swore then that you knew something about Charles's death. From the night you were out there, trying to keep an eye on Miles. I think you saw something...not a vision. You saw something with your *eyes*."

Wanda gave her a startled look, then glanced away.

"Wanda! Tell me what you saw!"

The psychic made a deep, rattling smoker's sigh. Then she said, "I saw Lee Woosley talking with Charles down at your dock. They was arguin'."

"Did you hear what they were arguing about? Did you see the murder?"

Wanda frowned. "Naw. I left. Figured I'd got my visions messed up. Didn't want to say nuthin' because I didn't want that guy to come after me and Dan. And I ain't had any visions about who done this. But I do get a feeling out of them. More than one."

Myrtle could guess what one of them would be. You didn't go hitting people over the head with gnomes and shovels unless you were *angry*.

"Anger is one," said Wanda, proving Myrtle right. "And the other is fear."

A potent combination, for sure.

Back at her house, Crazy Dan swiftly installed the motion detector lights. He put the extra keys on Myrtle's counter, then got his battered toolbox out to change out the locks on the doors.

Myrtle hesitated. "Oh—Crazy Dan. Can you come back in a few days and put those in?"

Wanda raised her penciled-in eyebrows at her and Myrtle was pleased that she actually did have the ability to surprise the woman.

"A few days?" asked Crazy Dan. "You might be dead by then."

"Yes, thank you, I'm well-aware of that fact. Nevertheless, that's what I'd like. Come back in a few days to do the work."

Crazy Dan closed up his toolbox, rolled his eyes at Wanda, and loped out to whatever beat-up vehicle had brought them here.

Wanda lingered for a moment. She rasped in her ruined voice, "Don't play games."

"Wanda, I'll stop you right there. I already know what you're going to say. *I'm in danger.* That's your usual broken-record prediction for me. But do you know what? I'm in danger just getting up every morning, even when there's not a murderer within two hundred miles of here. I'm in danger just stepping in and out of my shower and treading on throw rugs, and climbing staircases. It's not slowing me down, though, and I'm not going to live the short remainder of my life in fear of bathtubs *or* murderers." Myrtle raised her chin.

This time there was admiration in Wanda's eyes instead of trepidation. She nodded thoughtfully, then joined Crazy Dan to go home.

Myrtle got on her computer and wrote a blog post for the *Bradley Bugle*. It was a good thing Red never read the paper's blog, because he would hit the ceiling if he read this post.

Then Myrtle sat in front of *Tomorrow's Promise* and did chair exercises for thirty minutes. Because Wanda was right—she *was* in danger.

That night was uneventful and the following day was, too. Myrtle had planned on working on the case, but Elaine had asked her if she could watch Jack for her while she ran some errands. Jack had fallen asleep from sheer exhaustion after playing trucks with Myrtle for over an hour. While he napped, Myrtle wrote another quick story for the *Bradley Bugle*. There wasn't any news to report, but Sloan would get itchy if there weren't any updates.

In the middle of the night, Myrtle's motion detectors went off. Heart pounding, Myrtle grabbed her pepper spray and her cane. Keeping the lights off, she headed toward her kitchen window.

Peeking out into the yard, Myrtle saw Pasha the cat, blinking in the harsh lighting. But there *was* something dead in her yard again. A snake.

Myrtle opened her window to speak to the animal. "Pasha," she hissed. "Hope you're going to eat that."

Pasha looked noncommittally back at her.

Great.

Myrtle put the window down and decided to manually turn off the motion detectors for the rest of the night. One of her bedroom windows faced the backyard and the glow of the lights was going to keep her up all night. She wondered if she'd made an error in getting them installed. Pasha might be tripping them every night. Besides, if she was trying to trap this murderer, it really didn't make sense to use the motion detectors until after he was caught. The lights were sure to scare off any intruders.

She walked back to her bedroom and stared at the bed. Did she feel sleepy? No. As usual, she was wide awake. No point in thrashing around in the bed, failing abysmally at sleeping if you were completely awake. Her stomach growled. A midnight snack would be good. She glanced at the clock. Or, rather, a three o'clock snack.

Myrtle turned on her lights and made a pimento cheese sandwich. When there was a light tapping at her backdoor, she nearly jumped through the roof.

She picked up her pepper spray again and hurried to the door. It was Miles. "I saw your lights on," he said gruffly.

Myrtle held open the door, slumping in relief against the doorjamb. "You're not a killer," she muttered.

"Were you expecting one?" asked Miles mildly. Myrtle noticed that he appeared to be a bit flushed.

"Yes," said Myrtle. "As a matter of fact, I was. Killers seem to be using my backyard as a hangout. What brings you here?"

Miles was having a tough time making eye contact with Myrtle. He cleared his throat, paused, then cleared his throat again. Finally, he sighed. "I miss you."

Myrtle felt her mouth sag open and she snapped it shut, waiting to see what he might say next.

Miles took his glasses off and carefully cleaned a real or imagined smudge from them. "I'd always thought our friendship was sort of a one-way street. You seemed like you needed me more than I needed you—you needed somebody to visit with in the middle of the night, you needed a sounding board, you needed a ride, you needed a sidekick."

Myrtle nodded. It had felt unbalanced sometimes. Although she tended to ignore the imbalance, figuring Miles needed her too—somehow.

He cleared his throat again. "Yesterday, I had another ridiculously pointless and monotonous board meeting to go to."

Miles was on the board for several nonprofits. It drove him crazy, which made Myrtle wonder why he kept ending up on boards.

"After I was finally out of there, all I could think of was that I wanted to call you up so we could laugh at the pretentious people who ran the meeting," said Miles.

"The ones who love to hear themselves talk?" asked Myrtle. "And who use all that business jargon?"

"Where they blather on and on and never really say anything. At least, nothing that makes any sense," said Miles with another sigh.

"It does make a vapid meeting better when you can tear it apart with a friend afterward," said Myrtle thoughtfully.

"And I had to go to a dentist in Simonton," said Miles gloomily. "To have my tooth filled."

"Oh. I guess you didn't want to go to Dr. Bass."

"I *did* call Bass's office, actually. I had a follow-up visit planned for next week, but the tooth was starting to bother me so I tried to get worked in. But he was taking a couple of days off," said Miles. "So I went to another dentist. I realized that I was more relaxed going to the dentist when you were with me."

Interesting. He hadn't appeared all that relaxed when they'd gone to Dr. Bass's office. But she wasn't going to dissuade him from his fond remembrances.

"Plus, you got me hooked on that stupid show," muttered Miles.

"What's that?" asked Myrtle, blinking innocently.

"You made me addicted to that dumb soap opera of yours!"

"You mean *Tomorrow's Promise*?" asked Myrtle.

"Yes. And I feel terrible watching it by myself, because it's a guilty pleasure. I need you to watch it with me. Somehow it doesn't seem so awful to watch it when it's a group activity."

"Do two people make a group?" asked Myrtle in a doubtful voice. "I thought two people were just a couple."

"Then I kept wondering what was going on with the case. So you've even got me hooked on sleuthing." Miles held out a hand. "Can we be friends again?"

Myrtle solemnly shook his hand.

"And now that that's done," said Miles, "can you fill me in with what you're doing to nab the murderer? Because I'm sure you're probably close to doing so."

"Well, I've written a post for the *Bradley Bugle*'s blog revealing my investigative journalism was uncovering some important clues that seemed to lead to a particular individual. Then I added that once I pieced together all the parts of the puzzle, I would be sharing my findings with the state police and the *Bugle*'s readers would get a front-row seat for the show."

"I see," said Miles. "You're expecting whoever has been trying to scare you off to come back over and silence you for good."

"Something like that," said Myrtle. "But I technically wasn't expecting the murderer to try to kill me tonight because I scheduled the post to run tomorrow morning. And I'm very glad you came by because I was going to swallow my pride and ask you if you could be my backup tomorrow night."

For once, Miles didn't do any of the hemming and hawing that he usually did when Myrtle asked for his help with a case. He really *must* have missed being involved. "Sure," he said, "what do you need me to do?"

"Are you free tomorrow?" asked Myrtle.

"Sure—I don't think I have anything going on tomorrow."

"Do you want to have a sleepover?" asked Myrtle.

Miles frowned at her. "Making up is one thing, Myrtle, but pretending that we're six years old is something else."

"No, no, I mean could you come over here for a stakeout? After the post runs on the *Bugle* blog, and after I start blabbing about my progress around town tomorrow morning, I think the murderer might make another trip over to my house tomorrow night. That means I can catch him in the act, since I don't have any proof about my suspicions."

Miles said, "So you know who did it?"

"They're only suspicions. I'll know for sure tomorrow night. So, do you just want to pull an all-nighter? We could just hang out in the living room with the lights out. Maybe read with some book lights."

"Sounds exciting," said Miles, rolling his eyes. "Won't Erma find an excuse to come over so that she can spy on us and see if we're embroiled in a secret romance?"

"Nope. I've found a way to scare her off. Photo albums. She's apparently just as allergic to photo albums as she is to cats. Which is good, because my photo albums are always around and Pasha is unreliable."

"We might end up with all kinds of excitement," continued Myrtle. "So, if someone breaks into my house with the door key, you'll just duck out of sight. I'll have my pepper spray and my cane and you can surprise them when they get close. Does that sound reasonable?"

"I don't know if anything having to do with two elderly crimefighters attacking a murderer in the middle of the night is reasonable, but it's doable. What time do you want me to come over tomorrow evening?" asked Miles.

"Not too early, because this guy will probably come by in the middle of the night," said Myrtle.

"Well, or in broad daylight," said Miles. "What about Lee? He was killed at something like ten o'clock in the morning."

"But the murderer's goal was obviously not to be detected. And when was he most likely to go undetected? When everyone on this street was at Charles Clayborne's funeral. So I'm thinking this killer is clever enough not to want to show up at my house when the neighbors are still stirring and might look out their windows."

"You're thinking I should come over around eleven or so?" asked Miles.

"I think so. And just be very surreptitious when you do. Don't be jingling change in your pocket or whistling or anything like that."

"Like I ever do," said Miles with a sigh. And they both grinned at each other. Things were happily back to normal.

Chapter Seventeen

The next morning, Myrtle checked her computer. She saw that her blog post had indeed published as she'd scheduled it.

There was also another interesting post on the *Bradley Bugle*'s blog. Apparently, Connie Clayborne was offering a reward for information involving the murder of her son. Myrtle blinked. It was a reward for five thousand dollars. The best part of all was that Connie was only asking for information, not an arrest. Myrtle smiled.

There was a light tap at her front door. This was puzzling at around seven in the morning, but not nearly as scary as the unexpected knock on the door last night. Myrtle looked out the front window and saw Annette there, still in her scrubs.

"Hi, Miss Myrtle," said Annette. "I'm on my way home, so I can't come in to visit. But I just wanted to let you know real quick that I found my pocketbook so that you wouldn't feel you had to keep looking for it. It had slid under the front seat of the car and I couldn't see it."

Myrtle had completely forgotten about her pocketbook. But she quickly said, "Oh good! I'm so glad you found it." She noticed there were some dark circles under Annette's eyes. From working the night shift at the hospital? Or something else? "Is there something wrong?" she asked. "You look like you might have something else on your mind."

Annette shrugged. "It's probably nothing. It's just that Silas and I are still arguing about everything. We had an argument before I left for work last night, too. I kind of dread going home."

"What have y'all been arguing about...your relationship with Charles still?"

"That's at the bottom of every argument, even if it's technically not what we're fussing over," said Annette. "But last night, we did actually argue about Charles. During the argument, it came out that Silas had followed Charles the night he died." She shifted her weight uncomfortably.

"Did he say anything else after that? He didn't confess to killing Charles, did he?"

"Nothing like that. That's about the time that I stormed off to work, since I was going to be late if I didn't go ahead and leave. Plus, the whole conversation was making me feel sick. I still don't think that Silas could kill anybody, but it's bad enough that he was even *there* the night Charles died." Annette's face was pale and unhappy.

"Are you going to ask him about it when you get home? What time does Silas leave for work?" asked Myrtle.

"He usually goes in at nine o'clock, so I have some time. I was going to go to Bo's Diner, eat breakfast, and kill time until he leaves the house. No, I wasn't going to ask him any more about it—the whole conversation was making me feel sick. But I can't stand not knowing, either." Annette hesitated. "Miss Myrtle, I hate to ask you this. It's just that you seem very interested and helpful. Could you possibly....?"

"I'd love to!" said Myrtle in a rush. Then she decided that was inappropriately enthusiastic, so she edited herself to say, "I mean, of course I'd be happy to help you out and ask Silas what happened the night Charles was murdered. In fact, you might have seen my post on the *Bradley Bugle*'s site today—I'm really getting close to piecing together who's behind these murders."

Annette wrinkled her brow as if she couldn't quite imagine why Myrtle would be investigating the murders to begin with. "I'm doing some investigative reporting for the paper. I'm a correspondent for them, you know."

"I didn't realize that, no," said Annette, still sounding dubious. "I don't read the paper very much—even online." Then her eyes widened with alarm. "You're not going to put anything about Silas in the paper, are you?" They got even bigger when another thought occurred to her. "Or tell Red about this?"

"No, I won't put a thing in the paper about it. And, believe me, I'm just trying to stay out of Red's way right now. He's convinced I need to be an inmate at the Greener Pastures retirement home. What's the best way for me to catch up with Silas? I know he's an electrician—does he spend much time at his shop, or is he on calls most of the time?"

"It depends. It might be better if you go ahead and run by there now, before he leaves for work," said Annette. "He usually gets ready right away and then just watches TV and eats cereal before he leaves, so you won't be interrupting his routine."

Annette took her leave and Myrtle got dressed quickly to go see Silas. She hesitated for a second, then called Miles. "I know it's early, but do you mind going with me to Silas Dawson's house?"

He hadn't minded much, but it had taken another ten minutes for him to get ready. By the time he pulled up in her driveway, Myrtle was getting worried that Silas would have already left before they got there.

"I understand about needing the ride to get to Silas's house quickly," said Miles in a mild voice as he sped away, "but why do you want me to go in with you?"

Myrtle snorted. "Because I think I've become completely paranoid. Somebody's playing with my head. They've come in my house, they've played obnoxious pranks, and they've killed people in my yard. So it crossed my mind that maybe Annette and Silas are setting me up to come over to their house to be murdered myself." She gave a short laugh that was tinged with hysteria.

Miles's eyes opened wide behind his wire-rimmed glasses. "You don't really think *that's* going to happen, do you?"

"Not really, but it was awfully convenient for Annette to happen by and ask me to ask Silas tough questions about the murder. It made me wonder, that's all. I'm sure she was genuinely looking for someone to listen to her and relieve her mind so that she didn't have to worry that she was living with a murderer," said Myrtle.

They pulled up into Silas's driveway, and Myrtle breathed a sigh of relief that his van was still there.

"What's your cover this time?" asked Miles quietly as they walked up the walkway. "You're not using that pocketbook story you were telling me about again, are you?"

"No, and that wasn't a story, anyway! It was true. No, I'm just going to tell him what I put on the blog this morning—that I'm writing an investigative report for the newspaper and could he answer a few questions for me," said Myrtle.

Miles looked uneasy. "I read that blog post, by the way. I thought that you were laying it on pretty thick, saying that you had almost pieced together who the murderer was and would be exposing him in the paper."

"Well, I had to lay it on thick so I could get him to come after me. I'm playing it safe, after all—you're coming over at eleven tonight and we're all prepared. And just in case our murderer...or murderers..."said Myrtle mysteriously, "don't read the paper's website, I'm going to spread the news verbally today, too."

Myrtle rapped on the door with her cane and Silas answered the door. He raised his eyebrows when he saw Myrtle. "More ugly pocketbooks to show me?" he asked. "Look, I've got to finish getting ready for work here. Can you make this snappy?"

Silas didn't appear to be in a wonderful mood. He gave Myrtle and Miles an irritated glare.

"You might not be aware of this, Silas, but I'm an investigative reporter on the staff of the *Bradley Bugle*."

Myrtle paused to let Silas fully absorb the importance of this position, but he looked supremely unimpressed.

She continued, a harder edge in her voice now. "I've been poking around in the murders of Charles Clayborne and Lee Woosley. A witness has put you near the scene of the crime slightly before Charles Clayborne was murdered. This witness said you were following the victim." There. It hadn't been necessary to mention Annette after all.

Silas bared his teeth and Miles made a loud, gulping sound, as if his throat had suddenly gone dry. "This witness wouldn't happen to be my wife, would it?"

Myrtle lifted her chin, looking down her nose at Silas. It was good to be tall, even if she'd been shrinking in recent years. "It would not. I'm not at liberty to reveal any information about my sources, however."

Somehow, the icy disdain and sense of authority that Myrtle was still able to channel, even after years of retirement from school teaching, was enough to convince Silas. "Yeah, I followed him the night he died. I didn't kill him, though."

"Why didn't you tell the police?" Miles ventured.

"Why do you think?" sneered Silas. "They'd have pegged the murder on me. And I didn't do it. My hat's off to the guy who did, though."

"What made you decide to follow Charles?" asked Myrtle.

"I was driving around kind of aimlessly, just trying to steady my nerves," said Silas. He stopped and looked at Myrtle's doubtful face. "Okay, it was more than just that. I was looking to see if I saw Annette's car anywhere it shouldn't be. I wanted to see what she was up to and if she was still having an affair with Charles. I spotted Charles walking toward your house," he nodded at Myrtle. "There was a woman following him. It was real shadowy, though, and I couldn't see who the woman was."

Myrtle frowned. "A woman *following* Charles? So it looked like they weren't together?"

"Well, I thought they were together, naturally. I parked my work van a short ways away so I wouldn't scare them off. I thought maybe I could get some proof that Annette hadn't stopped their relationship. But after I'd parked the van—wouldn't you know it?— I got a call from one of my regular customers on my cell phone. I finally got off the phone with him and started back where I'd last seen Charles and the woman."

He continued with a sigh. "When I got up to your yard, there was no sign of the woman. And Charles Clayborne was dead on the ground."

Myrtle drew in a sharp breath. "So...Annette..."

Silas cut her off right there. "Nope. Annette had an alibi. She was still working the day shift then and they held her over when her shift ended. So Annette was at the hospital in front of a bunch of witnesses when Charles Clayborne was killed."

So who was the woman?

"So who was the woman?" asked Miles, echoing her thoughts as they drove back home.

"I'm thinking it had to be Peggy Neighbors," said Myrtle. "She was the one who was so gaga over Charles. I can totally see her following him and trying to convince him that he needed to marry her—and be a dad to their daughter."

Miles nodded. "So then he rejected her again—possibly cruelly this time—and she hit him over the head with your Viking gnome?"

"Maybe. After all, she was probably pretty upset and frustrated," said Myrtle.

Miles pulled the car up into Myrtle's driveway. Puddin was crouched in Myrtle's front yard, over a gnome with a goofy grin that was holding a beer stein. "Okay, I give up," said Myrtle to Miles. "What do you think she's doing out there with my tipsy yard art?"

"I have a sneaking suspicion," said Miles with a grim face. "Knowing Puddin, this could be why people have been coming and going throughout your house, without breaking in."

Myrtle knitted her brows at that statement and peered harder out the car window. Puddin was now running her chubby hand on the ground around the drunken gnome. She had a puzzled expression on her face.

"Let me guess," said Myrtle through gritted teeth. "Puddin has been keeping a house key in my gnome's beer stein. Not *under* the gnome even, but in plain sight of anyone who happened to be paying even casual attention."

"And now," said Miles, "that key appears to be missing. Much to Puddin's surprise."

Myrtle pushed open the car door and fumbled with her cane. "Thanks for the ride, Miles. I'll see you tonight."

"Be careful, Myrtle," said Miles.

"Oh, I really don't think the murderer is going to come after me in broad daylight."

"No, I mean be careful not to get too mad at Puddin. You don't need a body in your *front* yard, too," said Miles.

"I'll be good," said Myrtle. It was more of a mantra than a promise. "I'm actually rather impressed that she showed up to clean of her own volition."

"She and Dusty must have run completely through their money on their vacation," said Miles dryly. "I think I hear the mower starting up in your backyard."

"Thank goodness. The grass was higher than my knees!" Myrtle slammed the car door behind her and thumped with her cane over to where Puddin was now on her hands and knees, looking around for the key.

"Lose something, Puddin?" growled Myrtle.

Puddin glared at her. "The key. Did you take it away? I was trying to clean up and your door was locked."

"No, I did *not* take it away, but I certainly would have if I'd known. Puddin, you do realize that anybody could see you out here taking a key and putting it back, don't you? So, if someone wanted to break into my house, you're giving them an easy way to do it."

Puddin looked down at her stubby fingers and started picking off her nail polish. "But you gave me a key so's I could clean up if you weren't here."

"I thought you'd put the key on your key ring!" Myrtle had a brain wave. "You did know that I could tell Red about this."

Now Puddin's expression was wary. She apparently had a couple of minor incidents some years ago, that made her watch her step around law enforcement. "How's that?" she asked, squinting her eyes in the sun.

"When you so conveniently put my key out on public display, someone took advantage of it. This individual has been entering my house, whenever he likes, for the past week. What you've done is aid and abet this criminal," said Myrtle.

Puddin looked as if she was puzzling out the vocabulary in that last sentence.

"You could get in trouble for helping out the person who broke into my house. Maybe Red would even think that *you* were the person who broke into my house. You've very familiar with my stuff, after all. And my valuables."

Myrtle's valuables consisted of a chipped Wedgewood bowl of her mother's, and an always-tarnished sterling porringer. But Puddin wouldn't know that.

Puddin turned even paler than her usual pasty complexion. "Don't tell Red, Miz Myrtle. What do you want me to do?"

With difficulty, Myrtle kept a straight face. "You could start by never hiding my key anywhere again. Not that you really hid it last time—you had it right out in the open."

Puddin nodded her head solemnly and crossed her heart with a pudgy finger.

"And you could start to really take some *effort* when you clean my house. Don't just push dust from one part of the table to the other. Don't just vacuum the very middle of the floor. Start putting your glasses on when you're cleaning...yes, I know you're doing housework half-blind! And sometimes I'm sure you didn't do a lick of housekeeping in a room—you just sprayed lemon furniture polish everywhere to make it smell clean."

Puddin looked somewhat abashed.

"And tell Dusty to be more pleasant to be around, while you're at it. And you be nice, too!" said Myrtle.

That old, familiar sullen look was stealing across Puddin's face, so Myrtle stopped while she was ahead.

Puddin considered Myrtle's words for a second or two, then nodded. "Okay. Dusty's out back cutting the grass."

If Myrtle had only known how easy blackmailing Puddin would be, she'd have done it years ago.

Chapter Eighteen

Peggy Neighbors was next on Myrtle's list of suspects to talk with. Myrtle was positive that it had been Peggy that Silas had seen the night Charles was murdered.

Peggy worked most days as a waitress at Bo's Diner in downtown Bradley. Myrtle waited until it was the middle of the afternoon, figuring that would be the slowest time at the diner, then made the short walk over.

A bell rang on the door when Myrtle pushed it open and the aroma of fried vegetables greeted her. Myrtle had lived in Bradley her whole life and one constant had been the diner, which never seemed to change. It had the same dark wood-paneled walls, the same green, Formica-topped tables and lunch counter, and the same scrubbed-clean look. The only change had been that young Bo took over the diner when his father died.

As she'd hoped, the diner was very quiet at almost three o'clock in the afternoon. And Peggy Neighbors was working today. Myrtle sat down and another waitress came up, so Myrtle asked if Peggy could possibly wait on her.

Peggy immediately came over. "Hi there, Miss Myrtle. How are things going? Clarisse said you asked for me to take care of your table?"

"If you could, Peggy. I was hoping to have a chance to ask you a few questions. Oh, and I'll have a pimento cheese dog." Myrtle had a fondness for this particular hot dog—coated with pimento cheese and served with a side of the diner's salty shoestring fries.

"Let me put that in for you and I'll be right back," said Peggy. A minute later, she was back and sat across from Myrtle in the booth. "I told Bo you were wanting to talk and he said it was okay for me to take a break. There's really no one in here now, anyway."

Bo had probably thought Myrtle was lonely and needed an ear. Fine. Whatever was going to get Peggy a break to talk to her for a minute. "Peggy, I don't know if you know this, but I write stories for the *Bradley Bugle*. I'm doing an investigation for the paper on Charles Clayborne's murder and I'm really making some progress. In fact, I'm putting the last pieces of the puzzle together, then I'm hoping to go to Red with it tomorrow."

Myrtle was pleased with the way she was spreading news of solving the mystery around. The murderer would come after her tonight, for sure.

Peggy had paled at the mention of Charles. Was that because she missed Charles so much, or because Myrtle said she was figuring out who killed him?

Peggy said, "No, I didn't really know that. Was that what you wanted to talk to me about?" Her brows were knitted in confusion.

"I did. Because while I was investigating, I heard one witness say that he saw you with Charles near the scene of the crime the night he was murdered."

Now Peggy's face was completely pale. "They must have been mistaken, Miss Myrtle."

"They were pretty positive," lied Myrtle, crossing her fingers under the table.

"I told Red and the state police that I was home with my daughter that night," said Peggy, but she didn't look Myrtle in the eye when she said it.

"And I'm sure that Natalie would back you up on that, too. You're her mama. But do you really want to put your child in the position of lying for you during a murder investigation?" Myrtle filled her voice with as much reproach as she felt she was able to pull off.

Peggy took a deep breath and let it out slowly, staring down at the table as if trying to figure out what she was going to say. "Okay. I was out there with Charles the night he died. But I didn't have anything to do with his death, Miss Myrtle—you have to believe me!"

"Why didn't you just tell the police that you were there? It doesn't look good to have lied about it," said Myrtle.

"Think about it," pleaded Peggy. "I'm a single mom. My mom has been dead for years and now Daddy is dead. Who would take care of Natalie if I were in prison? I decided not to say anything about it. After all, I knew I wasn't involved. And what would happen if the police just didn't believe me?"

"What happened that night?" asked Myrtle.

"I was trying to convince Charles to go out with me again," said Peggy in a small voice. "We'd dated back in high school and he'd told me back then that he planned to marry me after graduation. But he didn't," she continued bitterly. "Once we graduated, he moved away and left me behind in Bradley."

"With a baby," added Myrtle in a low voice.

Peggy gave her a startled look. "How did you know that?"

"Don't worry; it's not a rumor going around town or anything. I specifically talked to someone who knew the situation," said Myrtle.

Peggy relaxed, but her expression was still guarded. "So I had joined him at the bar where he'd been the last few nights. He wasn't really that friendly toward me—kept interrupting what I was trying to say to him to talk to somebody else. When he looked at his watch, he looked surprised at how late it was. Probably because he was so tipsy. He said he had to go and I followed him out. I wondered if maybe he was going to be meeting with another woman."

Myrtle cleared her throat. "I'm surprised you really wanted to get back together with Charles, Peggy. After all he'd done to you. And I thought you were starting to go out with Dr. Bass and starting on a new relationship."

Peggy gave a hoarse laugh. "No, Hugh and I weren't going out. That's just something my dad wanted for me so much that I half-started believing it myself. Even back when I was in high school, my dad kept telling me not to date Charles—that Hugh had a better head on his shoulders. Daddy told everybody that Dr. Bass and I were dating—even Charles. But there were no dates...just once when I sat down with Hugh in a booth when he came here to eat...just like we're doing now. Daddy was pleased as punch when he found that out."

"So Dr. Bass was even an eligible bachelor in high school. Sounds too good to be true." Myrtle knew how high school kids were from her teaching days. She was always suspicious of reports of angelic teenage boys.

Peggy nodded emphatically. "It *was* too good to be true. I kept telling Daddy that Hugh was just as wild as the other boys. He wasn't any better than Charles. He'd go out and play pranks just like they would—bashing mailboxes in, toilet papering the trees, egging houses and cars. It wasn't like Hugh was perfect or anything."

"Back to the night that Charles was murdered. He was on foot—is that right?" asked Myrtle.

"Yes, he hadn't wanted to stay with his mother, so he was in that motel just a few blocks away from downtown. But he wasn't heading in that direction. At first, I just stopped him in the parking lot of the bar. I told him that I wanted to make some kind of a future with him—to at least have him be involved in Natalie's life." Peggy's face fell. "He didn't want to listen. He just stomped right off. I followed him, still trying to get him to listen."

She hesitated, and Myrtle wondered if she were editing her story before she told it. "Like I said, I followed him to see where he was going. I wasn't thinking real straight. I was pretty far behind him so he wouldn't see me. I guess I thought that if I saw him meeting with another woman, I'd really tell them both off."

"By the time I caught up to where he was, he was in someone's backyard. It was your yard, Miss Myrtle. I knew that because of all the gnomes."

"You know I have a gnome collection?" asked Myrtle, raising her eyebrows in surprise.

"I think everybody in Bradley knows that, Miss Myrtle," said Peggy with the first hint of a smile that she'd shown since she sat down with her.

"Once I saw where he was, I wasn't so worried." Peggy flushed. "What I mean to say is that I knew that you and Charles weren't involved in a relationship or anything."

Myrtle gave a shudder. "Indeed not."

"Charles stood in your yard for a while, kind of swaying on his feet and staring at your house and the houses next to you. He almost looked like he was confused or didn't know which house he was going to. Then he walked from your backyard down the hill to your dock. He sat out there for a while. He had a bottle with him—a beer that he'd started drinking at the bar. The moon reflected on the lake and I could see him sitting there, drinking, and looking at the water."

Now it made sense why he'd been in her backyard. She'd wondered why Charles would have gone up to talk to Miles from the *back*. Even though he was drunk, it still seemed as if he'd have staggered up to his front, not his back door. He probably sat down at the lake, drank a little more, and finally screwed up enough courage to go up and persuade Miles to invest in his scheme.

"Somebody came up to join him. I couldn't hear what they were saying from where I was. But it looked to me like they were having an argument. They were both waving their hands around like they were mad," said Peggy.

"It was a man?" asked Myrtle, leaning over the table to listen closer. It must have been Peggy's father. Wanda had told her she'd seen them there.

"I don't know who it was," said Peggy hurriedly, looking away. "But I know that it was a man. I figured Charles was trying to do one of those business deals he was bragging about to everybody. Seems like that's all Charles wanted to talk about once he came to town—money."

"Did you see anybody else while you were near my house?" asked Myrtle, thinking of Silas. "Anybody coming, going or lurking?"

Peggy thought for a moment, then shook her head. "Now I've really got to go," she said quickly. "Things are starting to pick up in the diner again."

If *picking up* meant one additional customer, it was.

Myrtle had one more task she wanted to complete today...talk with Dr. Bass. She knew Miles wasn't planning on seeing Hugh Bass again, preferring to go to a dentist in another town. She rolled her tongue over her teeth. There didn't seem to be anything chipped, breaking off, or needing rearranging. She'd just go walk over to his office and wait in the parking lot for him to leave. The office always closed promptly at five-thirty.

Fortunately, she didn't have to loiter too long in the parking lot. There had already been a couple of concerned dental patients who'd come over to see if she was all right and needed anything. One of them seemed to suspect that she might be suffering from dementia and was determined to drop her off at Red's house. Myrtle finally dispatched her by being just a wee bit more caustic than she might ordinarily have been. That display of temper had been the only thing that convinced the Good Samaritan that Myrtle hadn't lost her faculties.

When Myrtle saw Pam-the-hygienist leave, she quickly ducked out of sight. Pam would call Red just to be mean, faking concern all the while.

Finally, Dr. Bass came out of the building, carefully locking the door behind him. He lifted his eyebrows in surprise when he saw Myrtle. "Mrs. Clover? We're closed right now. Are you having a problem? Why don't you call Pam tomorrow morning and make an appointment. Tell her I said I'd fit you in."

"You know, I really do appreciate that, Dr. Bass. But my teeth seem to be doing all right." Myrtle mentally knocked on some wood. All she needed was dental problems right now. "What I wanted to do, though, was ask you some questions."

Now there was a wary look in Dr. Bass's eyes. "Some questions?"

Myrtle nodded. "You might not know this, but I'm an investigative reporter for the *Bradley Bugle*."

Dr. Bass gave Myrtle a smile that he probably intended to show interest, but only succeeded in displaying condescension. "You mentioned that before."

"Oh. Well anyway, I've been looking into these murders and now I feel that I'm very close to putting the final pieces of the puzzle together. Once I do, I'll naturally go to Red and let him know I've solved the case."

Dr. Bass's lips pressed together into a thin line.

"But I am trying to tie up a few odds and ends. Take, for instance, your involvement in this case," said Myrtle.

"Oh, I wouldn't say that I have any involvement in the case," said Dr. Bass brusquely. "After all, this is a man that I knew back in high school. I'm sorry that he's dead, naturally."

"Dr. Bass, I know that you have more involvement with Charles Clayborne than that." Myrtle noticed the smirky smile of his had finally been wiped off his face. "I've learned that when you graduated from high school, you both moved away to the same town, went to the same college, and were even roommates while you were in medical school and afterward."

Hugh Bass shrugged. "It's a way of saving money, that's all." His gaze was sharp as he studied Myrtle.

"It just all flies in the face of what your position was—that you hadn't seen Charles for a number of years. You lied. I've also heard that you had an argument with Charles Clayborne a few days before he was murdered," said Myrtle.

Dr. Bass crossed his arms on his chest in a defensive posture. "We may have argued. I didn't kill the man, if that's what you're implying."

"What was this argument about?" asked Myrtle.

He still looked as though he was wavering, trying to decide how much to tell Myrtle. "None of this is going in the newspaper, right?"

"Dr. Bass, right now I'm just trying to figure out what happened." That was the truth, after all. No need to scare the man off before he gave her information.

"We argued, because Charles was trying to force me into investing in this shady-sounding business deal that he was setting up," said the dentist with a sigh. "It was obviously some kind of scam or a pyramid scheme or something like that. Of course, I didn't want anything to do with it. And Charles was convinced that *this* time, this deal was going to be the one to finally make him rich. I told him that the best way to get rich was to pick something you're good at and invest a whole lot of time and sweat into it every day. It wasn't the kind of advice that Charles liked to hear," said Dr. Bass. "He started letting me have it. That's probably what your witness saw—Charles arguing with *me*, instead of the other way around."

"Why did he think that he could persuade you to invest in something you so clearly wanted nothing to do with?" asked Myrtle innocently. Would he tell her that Charles was trying to blackmail him? A past incarceration and a revoked dental license, even in another state, certainly wouldn't be easy for the town of Bradley to swallow.

The wary look was back on Dr. Bass's face. He grew suddenly busy digging his car key out of his pocket. "We grew up together, remember?

There were plenty of instances of youthful immaturity that I'm sure Charles could use to persuade me."

He clearly still wasn't inclined to talk about the past. "Did you finally convince him that you weren't going to invest?" asked Myrtle. "How did you leave it?"

The dentist said, "No, Charles was the kind of guy who was never convinced. He was going to keep talking to me about the scheme, for sure. He told me even this really straight-laced, retired cousin of his was planning to invest."

Finally, some confirmation why Charles was trying to talk to Miles. Charles had clearly presumed he could sucker Miles into investing in the scheme. Who knows if Miles would have been able to, if that meeting had happened? Miles could be a real softy.

BACK AT HOME THAT EVENING, Myrtle tried to relax, but a wave of excitement kept streaking through her. She'd done a great job spreading the news around town today that she was on the verge of solving the case and telling Red the name of the culprit. She'd set herself up for an intruder tonight. Plus, she'd been smart and covered her bases. She had pepper spray, a pot of coffee to keep her awake, and a friend coming over. She was in good shape.

At nine o'clock, Myrtle realized she should turn off her lights. What intruder would try to attack her when all her lights were on? And the intruder that she strongly suspected would arrive tonight was definitely not stupid. She also made sure the motion detector lights were still turned off. And she locked her door—she didn't want the murderer to realize she'd laid a trap.

Then Myrtle unlocked her front door so that Miles could come quickly in at eleven and so that she could quickly *exit*, if she needed to. She put some pillows in her bed to make her appear to be under the covers. Then she pulled the covers over the pillows. It *sort* of looked like a sleeping figure. In the dark, she thought it would pass. She certainly didn't want to be in the bedroom with the killer, though—there really would be no way out.

Instead, Myrtle took a large cup of coffee into the living room with her and put a chair right outside the kitchen door. That way, she could hear when someone was coming in through the back door.

Myrtle wasn't quite ready to stand guard in that chair yet—it was still very early. She figured she'd sit on the living room sofa and read her book with a book light until Miles came over, then she'd move to her guard post.

At ten o'clock, she thought she heard a scraping sound outside her back door. She frowned. Miles was supposed to be coming in through the front. Besides, it was too early for Miles to be coming over.

Myrtle froze as she strained her ears to hear. Sure enough, the metallic, scraping noise came again.

Someone was trying to unlock her back door in the dark.

Chapter Nineteen

Myrtle grabbed her pepper spray at the same moment the back door creaked open. She carefully peeked around the kitchen door and saw the intruder entering her bedroom—clearly someone who'd become familiar with her house from previous break-ins.

She thought about picking up the phone to dial Red...or Miles, but knew there wouldn't be enough time. Those pillows in her bed wouldn't fool Hugh Bass for very long.

There was a slashing sound coming from her bedroom and Myrtle's breath caught in her throat. It sounded like stabbing.

There was a frustrated cry and Hugh Bass bolted from her bedroom...and saw Myrtle on the other side of the kitchen island. He held up his knife and charged at her. Myrtle waited, blood pounding in her head, until he came close. Then she lifted the bottle of pepper spray and directed a steady stream right at his face.

With a howl of pain, Dr. Bass dropped to his knees, digging at his eyes with his fingers. Myrtle quickly grabbed the knife and threw it across the room. She desperately looked around her—looking for something that she could use to knock the dentist unconscious before he charged her again.

Then she jerked open the freezer, pulling the fifteen pound, rock-hard ham to the very edge of the bottom freezer shelf with some difficulty. Then she dropped it right on Dr. Bass's head.

It was a knockout punch.

Myrtle ended up calling Miles next. She still had so much adrenaline coursing through her that apparently whatever she said to him was quite garbled. He interpreted it as, "Call Red and come over," which is exactly what he did.

It was good, for once, that Red lived so close to Myrtle. That's because Dr. Bass started stirring after only a few minutes. She retrieved her cane from the living room and perched on a kitchen stool, ready to strike with the cane if he should stop being groggy and start attacking her again.

But once Red and Miles ran in, she decided that she'd take to her favorite chair in the living room. She appeared to have a case of the shakes. She poured herself a sherry—just to steady her nerves. As an afterthought, she brought the bottle with her into the living room.

The state police weren't far behind. There were pictures taken in the kitchen and samples of things taken outside. They found a key to Myrtle's door in Dr. Bass's pocket, where he'd hastily stuck it before entering Myrtle's bedroom. Myrtle told the police where they could find the knife he'd tried to kill her with. Then, of course, there was the fact that Dr. Bass was curiously dressed completely in black, even with a black cap and black gloves.

None of those things would have pointed to evidence that Dr. Bass had broken into Myrtle's house. But fortunately, something had loosened Dr. Bass's tongue. He might have been tired of his secrets and relieved to tell them—or it might have been that the frozen ham had made him temporarily lose his mind. At any rate, he was confessing to the police, who hastily informed him of his rights.

Miles was drinking sherry out of one of Myrtle's bathroom cups, since the kitchen was occupied by police. "I guess we miscalculated when Dr. Bass would arrive. By the way, were you expecting *him*? I mean—had you already figured out that he'd killed Charles and Lee Woosley?"

"It was," admitted Myrtle reluctantly, "a miscalculation. It's lucky I was prepared for trouble the way I was. I was expecting Dr. Bass, yes. But I didn't realize he was coming by boat. If I'd thought about it, then I'd have pushed back the time that you were to join me. Oh—and Dr. Bass didn't kill Charles."

Miles's mouth gaped open and closed. It wasn't an attractive look for Miles.

Myrtle wasn't sure which part of her statement he was reacting to. "You see, Dr. Bass also lives on the lake. He wouldn't want to risk being seen approaching my house from the street, then cutting through someone's backyard. He did that one time and all Erma's motion detector lights went off. By arriving in a small boat, he just quietly pulled up to my dock and came up through the woods, directly to my backyard."

Miles had finally regained his speech. "Okay, I've got that. But...Dr. Bass didn't kill Cousin Charles?"

"Oh no. Lee Woosley killed Charles. Then Dr. Bass killed Lee Woosley."

"But why? I mean, I understand why Lee would murder Charles—he'd treated his daughter horribly in the past and was treating her just as poorly when he returned to town. I just can't see why Dr. Bass would want to kill Lee, though," said Miles.

"I'll tell you what I think happened, Miles. Then Red will be able to confirm my deductions, since it sounds like Dr. Bass is confessing to everything he can think of in there. Peggy Neighbors had tried to get Charles back in a relationship with her. She told him about their daughter. He wanted nothing to do with Peggy or his daughter. His daughter is finishing up high school and Peggy probably needs the financial help to get her through college. That's exactly the kind of problem that Charles wouldn't have wanted. Peggy was upset and told her father what happened...I guess she must have phoned him. Lee decided to confront Charles," said Myrtle.

Miles nodded. "That all makes sense. But where does Dr. Bass come in?"

"I'm getting there! So Lee has an argument with Charles out on the dock. Wanda saw it with her own eyes. In the course of the argument, he tells Charles that Peggy doesn't need him anyway—he's not good enough for Peggy. Peggy is, in fact, going to start dating the most eligible bachelor in town...Dr. Hugh Bass."

Miles looked doubtful at this. "Peggy Neighbors and Dr. Bass? I don't really see the two of them together. Peggy is very *nice*, but...."

"Exactly. So Charles's reaction to this, when the two men are down at the dock having this discussion, is to laugh. He not only laughs at Peggy's prospects with Dr. Bass, but he laughs at the fact that Lee thinks he's so eligible. Charles would have sneered at that, telling Lee that Dr. Bass was actually a former convict and even had his dental license revoked."

Miles nodded. "So the men, as you mentioned, are down at the dock. They're arguing. How does Charles end up dead in your yard?"

"At some point, Charles walks away. His plan is to talk to you about some kind of scheme he wants you to invest in. He's been drinking a lot remember. So he staggers off to your yard, although he ends up in mine. Lee follows him up, still furious at the entire situation and enraged by what Charles has told him. Charles is an expert at enraging people," said Myrtle.

"And he bashes Charles over the head with your Viking gnome," said Miles.

Myrtle said, "Breaking it with the force. It was the only heavy object available to him at the time. I think Peggy even saw her father there—she must have, since she was following Charles. I bet she'll end up telling Red and the state police what she saw."

Miles took a thoughtful sip of his sherry, draining the bathroom cup. "So, let's see. This means that somehow Lee talked to Dr. Bass. Almost immediately. Did he try to blackmail the dentist, do you think?

Squeeze some money out of him? I'm sure that, as a handyman, he couldn't have been bringing in much income. He probably helped support Peggy and his granddaughter, too."

Myrtle shook her head. "Well, I don't know for sure. Red might, since Dr. Bass is spilling everything in there. But I can't imagine Lee Woosley caring about money enough to blackmail. He was sort of a softie, I think. And old-fashioned. I think he was affronted that Dr. Bass was practicing dentistry in Bradley after what he'd done in West Virginia. I believe he approached Dr. Bass about it, the day before he was murdered. Maybe he even gave him an ultimatum—get out of town or I'm going to tell Red about this."

Miles said slowly, "Then Lee returned to your house during the funeral to finish up the job he'd started for you before everyone came by for the reception."

"And Dr. Bass followed him there. No one was around, after all—the whole town was at the funeral. It was the perfect time to get rid of Lee Woosley. Dusty had even conveniently left him a shovel outside to beat him over the head with. Then he really just had to stay out of the way and act as he normally did. Except he couldn't resist coming back to see if he'd accidentally left some clue behind or if he'd been discovered. Elaine snapped a picture of him in the area."

Miles said, "I can definitely see him doing all of that. But I don't understand what he was doing throwing eggs at your house. And messing around with your things."

"I think Dr. Bass was trying to shake me up and rattle me so much that I would stop nosing around in the case. Peggy even mentioned that he ran with a crowd in high school that liked playing pranks—rolling trees and egging houses and that kind of thing. As far as his breaking into my house, I think there were a couple of different things he was trying to do. He has to drive right past my house to get from his house to his office. He obviously must have noticed Puddin putting the key away at some point and took it...probably thinking that he might need to silence me for good at some point."

"Makes sense. But you told me that someone had been inside your house during the daytime. And Dr. Bass works during the day."

"He does. But you told me he'd taken a couple of days off and you'd had to go to your dentist in Simonton. One of those days was when my house was broken into. I'd guess he was also trying to figure out what progress I was making on the case—he knew I was investigating. He might have looked for notebooks where I wrote about the murders or for a journal. To top it all off, he put things in weird places while he was in here just to make me doubt myself," said Myrtle.

"Good thing it didn't work," said Miles.

Myrtle didn't answer. She didn't want to admit that Dr. Bass had made her start wondering if she was losing her memory.

Miles gave a satisfied sigh. "This is actually a very satisfactory end to the case, Myrtle. Justice for everyone. Lee Woosley paid for Charles's life with his own. Hugh Bass has been arrested and will pay for murdering Lee and for operating a dental office without a license. Everything is back to normal again."

As Dr. Bass was driven away, Myrtle had to agree.

Actually, thought Myrtle the next morning, everything was *better* than normal. She put her feet up on an ottoman as Puddin demurely cleaned her house, putting some real elbow grease into the process for once.

Dusty was mowing the grass...*again*. Although it really didn't need it. He'd even trimmed her bushes this morning.

Crazy Dan and Wanda had returned, and Crazy Dan was deftly replacing the locks on Myrtle's doors. Wanda had already reminded her to turn her motion detector lights back on.

The icing on the cake had really come when Miles's Aunt Connie insisted on giving Myrtle the reward for information on her son's death. Myrtle had put up some modest attempts at turning down the check, but had rapidly been convinced she needed to take it. She used some of the money to buy a new camera for Elaine.

Myrtle's front-page story for the *Bradley Bugle,* covering the attempted attack on her life and the arrest of the killer was a spectacular success and a top-selling issue for the newspaper. It even got picked up on the AP wire. Elaine's picture of Dr. Bass talking with Lee Woosley accompanied the story and gave it the finishing touch it needed.

Red was talking to a contractor about putting a privacy fence in her backyard. He decided he needed to prevent her yard from becoming a popular crime spot in the future. The privacy fence meant that Erma would no longer be gaping at her when Myrtle was trying to have a quiet moment outside.

Best of all might have been the moment, a few minutes ago; when Miles knocked on her door...bearing a smile, his tape of the latest *Tomorrow's Promise,* and a brand-new Viking gnome.

About the Author:

Elizabeth writes the Southern Quilting mysteries and Memphis Barbeque mysteries for Penguin Random House and the Myrtle Clover series for Midnight Ink and independently. She blogs at ElizabethSpannCraig.com/blog, named by Writer's Digest as one of the 101 Best Websites for Writers. Elizabeth makes her home in Matthews, North Carolina, with her husband. She's the mother of two.

Sign up for Elizabeth's free newsletter to stay updated on releases: https://elizabethspanncraig.com/newsletter/

This and That

I love hearing from my readers. You can find me on Facebook as Elizabeth Spann Craig Author, on Twitter as elizabethscraig, on my website at elizabethspanncraig.com, and by email at elizabethspanncraig@gmail.com.

Thanks so much for reading my book...I appreciate it. If you enjoyed the story, would you please leave a short review on the site where you purchased it? Just a few words would be great. Not only do I feel encouraged reading them, but they also help other readers discover my books. Thank you!

Did you know my books are available in print and ebook formats? And most of the Myrtle Clover series is available in audio. Find them on Audible or iTunes.

Interested in having a character named after you? In a preview of my books before they're released? Or even just your name listed in the acknowledgments of a future book? Visit my Patreon page at https://www.patreon.com/elizabethspanncraig.

I have Myrtle Clover tote bags, charms, magnets, and other goodies at my Café Press shop: https://www.cafepress.com/cozymystery

If you'd like an autographed book for yourself or a friend, please visit my Etsy page.

I'd also like to thank some folks who helped me put this book together. Thanks to my cover designer, Karri Klawiter, for her awesome covers. Thanks to my editor, Judy Beatty, for all of her help. Thanks to beta readers Amanda Arrieta and Dan Harris for all of their helpful suggestions and careful reading. Thanks, as always, to my family and readers.

Other Works by the Author:

Myrtle Clover Series in Order (be sure to look for the Myrtle series in audio, ebook, and print):

Pretty is as Pretty Dies

Progressive Dinner Deadly

A Dyeing Shame

A Body in the Backyard

Death at a Drop-In

A Body at Book Club

Death Pays a Visit

A Body at Bunco

Murder on Opening Night

Cruising for Murder

Cooking is Murder

A Body in the Trunk

Cleaning is Murder

Edit to Death

Hushed Up (late 2019)

Southern Quilting Mysteries in Order:

Quilt or Innocence

Knot What it Seams

Quilt Trip

Shear Trouble

Tying the Knot

Patch of Trouble

Fall to Pieces

Rest in Pieces

On Pins and Needles

Fit to be Tied

The Village Library Mysteries in Order (Debuting 2019):

Checked Out

Overdue (late 2019)

Memphis Barbeque Mysteries in Order (Written as Riley Adams):

Delicious and Suspicious

Finger Lickin' Dead

Hickory Smoked Homicide

Rubbed Out

And a standalone "cozy zombie" novel: Race to Refuge, written as Liz Craig

.

CPSIA information can be obtained
at www.ICGtesting.com
Printed in the USA
LVHW051300310520
657047LV00012B/381

9 780983 920885